Paint by Murders

Book One of the
Emily Ellis Series

AMANDA JAEGER

Paint by Murders

Editor: Genevieve A. Scholl
Cover Design: Troy Cooper
Formatted by: Genevieve A. Scholl

TABLE OF CONTENTS

Art: The expression of creative skill and imagination.
Art for Art's Sake: The idea that the purpose of art is the self-expression of the artist who creates it.

Content Warning: Sexual Assault

PROLOGUE

Her scent fills me up like city tap water in a dirty glass. It's a mixture of gritty coconut and salt. I hate it when they cry. It's so irritating. So I bite back my distaste and put my hand on her cheek to caress her creamy skin.

Women like touches like that, you know. Especially the young ones. It's a sense of security they never had with their deadbeat dads and the carousel of boyfriends who never bothered to give them the attention they crave. So I give it to them. I touch them. I make sure they have everything they need to scream my name out like splattered paint in the wind. Because if they give themselves — their talent — to me, then I know I'll have a seat reserved in The Circle calling my name.

But she doesn't seem to like it this time. She turns her head down, looking at the floor instead of my eyes. That won't do. My hand pulls her chin up and I force her gaze to meet mine.

"There, there. That's better." I make the cooing sound all the girls fall for with little-big eyes that scream, "I'm yours for the taking, as long as I can have you, too."

"You're a monster!" she spits back, but it's okay.

I know she's scared, and sometimes scared girls yell. I just need to make her understand she doesn't have to be scared. Not with me. I care for her because I care for what she can do with her magical hands. They make such pretty things, and I want to own those pretty things and the talent they came from. I want to be able to witness her gift and let the world see it, too. If she can just let me in...

My fingers rake through her auburn hair. It's so freaking soft, like mink or fox fur. Her bare body squirms under me, trying to find its way free, but I pull her back. There's no way I'm letting my soft minx go. Not without what I need.

"What do you want with me?" Her voice sounds like a siren. It's loud and piercing, and if we weren't in this basement, hidden away from the rest of the living world, I'd be concerned someone might hear.

I mean, she should know better. She's been here before and plenty loud. She isn't one of the quiet ones. She has never bitten her lip or tongue or my shoulder to keep herself silent. But no matter how much she screamed and cried and begged for more, no one has ever come knocking to check on us.

"Shhhh." I hold a finger up to her pillowy lips. "No need for any of that, now." And there really isn't any need. It's just me. I'm inches away. I can easily hear her if she were to talk to me in a whisper instead.

She spits. She literally pulls back the saliva and phlegm in her throat and forces it out of her mouth and onto my finger. Some of it flies past my finger and lands across my cheek and down the bridge of my nose. Disgusting. I wipe the sticky substance away with my sleeve. When I meet her eyes, I can tell she's afraid of what I'm going to do with my fist.

I'll go ahead and bask in the control I know I have a little longer. It feels good, warm. Like golden sunshine on my skin.

But even though my fist is clenched and pulled back, I'd never use my fist on her. That's too bold, too brutal, too violent. Why would I ever want to deface the person who holds so much I want?

I smile and lean into her. I can push past the smell of salt and take in the scent of her skin on her neck. The coconut is strong here, like she forgot to rinse off the body wash behind her ears. My mouth instinctively reacts, salivating in puddles because it smells so sweet. I want so badly to know if her skin tastes as good as her scent, so I run my tongue from her clavicle to her chin to find out.

I'm right. It is sweet, but not in the fake coconut kind of way. In a way that makes me think of lily pads and cotton, though it tastes more like cream.

Her body shivers and squirms under me. She's not a minx anymore; she's an octopus. Arms and legs are everywhere. I catch a quick glimpse of her nails. They're usually long and bright, and most of them still are. They're painted electric blue with a coat of glitter. But one is jagged and broken. She flails some more and I watch another nail chip on the floor, leaving behind a small streak of electric blue. She screams and grunts and tries to shift out from under me. Then, those octopus arms and legs move some more.

All I can think of is last week when those same arms and legs wrapped around me. She would have wrapped them around me twice, if she could. They pulled me into her deeper, calling my name as loud as she's screaming now. She enjoyed her shudders and shivers, asking for more. Actually, come to think of it, she never asked.

She *begged*.

They always did. They fell into my arms quickly and just as soon would fall on their knees, physically dying not to have the touch of my fingers on any — on *every* — part of their skin.

But now those shivers come with squirms, and I'm losing my patience with this one. I take a deep breath. It takes everything within me to hold onto the last ounce of patience I have and whisper into her ear, just like all the times I did before when it would set her off the edge and make her ready for me.

"You want to know what I want with you? I want *you*. I have always wanted *you*." My knees have found her thighs, and they do their job to spread them apart for me.

Her mouth says, "No," but she doesn't really mean it. Not when she's letting her legs move to the sides of me.

11

Silly girls are always like that. Saying one thing with their verbal language and another with their body language. It's a good thing I know how to read the correct one, the correct message they put out into the world.

The correct one is always their body.

And it always wants me. Just like I want her, here. Now.

"You have a talent," I whisper as I grind up on her, making sure it's slow and deliberate so her body responds with the correct language again. "And I need to hold that talent. I need to have it."

Her cheeks turn lemonade pink and I know that I did it right.

"I need to see inside of you. Find where that talent is." I arch my body deliberately again and watch her body react. Proof I was reading her right. Not that I needed proof. Experience is a great teacher, and I'm full of enough of it to be the professor of experience myself.

"Your magic hands. Your magic mind. You have something I have never had the pleasure of having before, and I need it."

Up. Down. Up. Down. Back and forth. I'm a smooth pendulum that's passing the time by clocking the natural rhythm of us.

Her body arches and her eyes roll back in her head. My own body language tells her everything she needs to hear and feel in order to be completely in this moment, and away from whatever is in her head that is fighting me off.

Silly women and their silly brains.

As I watch her body move in the exact ways I expect, I reach to the side of us on the floor. A pair of scissors lay there. They had fallen out of my pocket in her first bout of squirming and screaming. I left them there knowing eventually she would exhaust herself, relinquish herself to me.

The handle of the scissors is cold in my hand, but warms up quickly. And on one more arch of her body, I grab onto a handful of that minxy auburn hair and snip.

My entire body relaxes. It's in my hand now. A piece of her and her talent is now in my hand and I can use it. I can access it. Call onto it whenever I can and put it to use in my own hands. Or in the hands of whoever can benefit me.

She drops to the ground. Her head hits the concrete and nearly bounces back into place. I look at her body twist into an S shape as she holds her arms across her naked form.

I can do better, be better, craft better because of her. I should be thankful. I should worship this girl on my basement floor. But I look at her and everything in me tells me that worship is too strong of a word. Nothing of this *thing* on my floor deserves worship. *It* isn't helpful anymore. Not now that I snipped off what I needed.

It doesn't even deserve praise. It's naked and shaking with tears, and it's curling up into a little peach-colored ball on the floor.

This body language is saying something else entirely. It's saying, "make it stop." But there's nothing to stop. Not really. I'm off of it. Nothing is touching it. Nothing is happening to it. It's just existing.

So I guess I need to stop that. Stop it from existing.

I walk over to the little gas stove. The counter next to it holds a couple of water bottles and a ziplock baggie full of white powder. My magic powder that helps me dispose of whatever *things* I need out of my way.

I crack open the lid of one of the water bottles and unzip the bag. Just a little bit is all I need — all *it* needs — so I tap a little of the powder into the now open water bottle, close it up, and shake. The powder dissolves nicely. No trace of it is left behind.

Behind me, it whimpers. I turn around. It really is sad looking. It's like a stray dog after it has been hit by a car, off to the side and begging for mercy. So I walk up to it and kneel down, handing it a bottle of mercy.

From there, I'll let nature take its course. Maybe 24 hours. *It* hasn't eaten in a few days, at least nothing I've tried to feed it, so I'm sure it'll take less than that.

As it drinks from the mercy bottle, I find my pants that had been pulled off halfway across the room. I step into them and zip up. The lock of hair finds its way into my pocket for safekeeping. I pat the lump in my pocket and promise to put it to use soon.

I also find the other set of clothes. The set *it* was wearing, and I throw them over to the peach-colored ball on the floor. They plop down on the cement, so I figure it knows they're there. I figure the clothes will make their way back onto its body eventually.

I watch it chug down the bottle of water. Its wet cheeks are flushed and puffy. When the last drop hits its mouth, I smile.

"Thank you for your talent." The least I could do is say thank you, even though it'll never see how its talent would be used later.

And I leave it on the floor, with a confused look on its face. I walk up the uneven steps that came with this place. I hit the fourth step and lean to the sturdier side. When I get to the top of the steps, I take a deep inhale. It's time to give *it* some privacy. I'll come back later. Let *it* out. Let *it* go back home. Or, part of the way home. *It* may not even get there. *It* will probably only get to a few blocks by then and my mercy will take place.

So, I close the pull door when I reach the top step, making it flush with the floor. The washing machine eases back over it, concealing any trace of a door being there at all. I think I can hear some muffled noises behind that door, but they don't matter. I'm just giving some privacy, that's all. And time.

CHAPTER ONE

The Melting Clock House

"You sure you know what you're doing, Emily Ellis?" Livvy asks me with puppy dog hazel eyes.

I wince at the sound of my full name. I don't know why she insists on using it when she's all kinds of stressed out. It's like she's trying to be my mom or something, which is freaking annoying. And it stresses me the heck out, too.

I'd much rather her call me Mills. Like she does when she's not stressed.

Heck, I'd rather everyone calls me Mills. I've always felt like the nickname suits me much more than *Emily*.

"About as sure as anything else." Which is true. I don't always think things through, but once I start, I am sure as hell not going to stop. Even when it comes to fixing appliances I have no business opening up and poking around in.

We both grab hold of the front of the washing machine and step a foot back for balance.

"One, two, three."

We pull. Nothing happens.

"Freaking crap!" I yell and kick the washing machine hard. I bite back the sting in my toe, and the sound echoes throughout my mostly empty house. It's a crap house, with a broken-warped clock hung front and center in the front room — like a melting clock from Salvador Dali's painting — but I kind of love it. It's mine, at least for the time being. All mine. Even if it is mostly a dump.

Stupid band-aid fixes the owner left behind have me doing more work than I should be. And because I signed the contract without so much as glancing at the fine print, I'm left fixing appliances on my own. Here I am pulling apart a broken washer with a load of clothes that stopped washing in the middle of a cycle. My favorite pair of pants are in there, just mildewing away unless I can fix this thing.

"Maybe we should call a repairman?" Livvy looks at me, hopeful.

She's the kind of girl who wants to do things the right way every time, rather than play around. Seems silly to me as a double major in both biology and chemistry. Isn't that what scientists do? Play around until they find the solution they're looking for? But that's just who she is. She's the calm to my storm. She's what will get me to think through the next step, before I end up kicking a hole in the wall and having to pay whoever actually owns this place for damages.

I can't afford to call someone up to fix this thing. Not with almost every last penny of my bank account going into this place. Nope. I'm going to fix it myself.

I shake my head. "No; we're not calling on anyone except Dr. Google. He's free and we're smart. We can take care of this."

"Can we at least call Stark?"

Stark is Livvy's older brother, who looks just like her with dark skin, curly hair that pokes out in the front, and eyes that tell me he's always been full of both humanity and chutzpah. The Landon kindness genes must be strong in that family. The only difference is, Stark has more experience under his belt. And if I'm being honest, he's also a lot more handsome.

Not that Livvy isn't a looker. She is. She's just not my type.

Stark's real name is Anthony, but somewhere along the line, he got people to drop his real name for something a little edgier. People went along with the name Stark and he never looked back at his birth name again.

As I shake my head, I hope Livvy doesn't decide to actually call him over. "Livvy, we've *got* this. We're no damsels and we are not in distress." What I don't say is that I can't bear to see the look of pity on his face with us fighting to do something we had no business doing in the first place.

With a hand on my hip, I step back to take a hard look at the thing in front of me. This white magic box that has lost all its magic. My foot kicks at it again — *ouch* — willing the magic to come back.

"Hey, Livvy, go get me a butter knife. Should be in one of those boxes on the floor over there." My thumb points to a few unpacked boxes on the kitchen floor.

"You've been here for a week and you still haven't unpacked your utensils? What do you eat with?"

I throw both of my hands up in the air and wiggle my fingers. "I was born with these suckers. My experience says they work just as well as anything else, if not better."

Livvy shakes her head as she digs into one box, sets it aside, and starts on another. Eventually, she finds a butter knife and hands it to me. It's one I stole from Volga University's dining hall when I was a student. I slide the knife under the face of this washing machine from Hell and lift it up.

A loud pop reverberates in my ears and it's so exciting that I shout out loud, "Hell yes!" The knife slips easily on the other side and a second pop makes my insides giddy. Freaking yes, this is going to work.

"Here." I shove the stolen knife over to Livvy. "Go put this away and we'll try again."

"Away as in back in the box or away as in where it should go? In the utensil drawer?"

"Oh, shut up. Just put it down somewhere and grab a corner."

17

She chooses the countertop, and now with the both of us on either side of the washing machine, we pull. Hard.

Miracles must be real because the front of the machine pulls off like a large hinge and we're left with a white barrel full of soaking-wet jeans. I probably should have taken those out before we got to this point, but here we are. And there they are. A silent anti-mildewing prayer runs through my head and I hope it's enough to actually fix this thing and save my clothes.

"Holy crap, look at that thing." Livvy steps back to take a look at our handiwork, and I can see fear that could pass as excitement creep into her eyes. I knew all it would take is one big thing to go right for her to realize this was totally possible. Two independent girls without a single piece of appliance knowledge could figure out how to dismember a machine.

She quickly reaches back in her pocket and pulls out her phone. Her brown-skinned digits race feverishly to unlock the screen and pull open the tutorial video we had paused earlier.

"Okay, you see that hose underneath? It's connected to a weird-looking plastic box? You need to clamp that hose shut and see if there's anything inside that box."

I reach for the clamplike tool on the floor in front of me. It was part of a toolset left behind by whoever was here before me, so I have no idea what it's called or what its real purpose is. But it looks like a wrench and can clamp down like a lobster on steroids. I shove that sucker on the hose and tighten it up, pull off the little white box, and watch water spit out of both ends.

"Ugh!" I hate it when there's an unintended mess on my hands. But when the water stops, I look inside. The culprit is obvious. There's a ball of hair the size of Texas shoved inside. "Bingo!" A pair of pliers untangles and pulls the thick glob out easily. It drops to the floor like a dead rat after being fished out of a sewer.

Livvy dances her feet backward to avoid the mess as if the residue it collected was contagiously sickening. "Ew!" After squinting her eyes for a minute, she follows up with, "I guess keratin clumps can really get into everything, huh?"

"I guess so," I reply, but my eyes aren't on the ball of wet hair anymore. They're underneath the hair and around the hair, where the edges of a square are cut out on the floor. Two hinges lay flat, almost flush to the wood in the back, and by my knees and toward the front is a little knotted rope. It sticks up like a little piece of taunting suspicion.

"What the heck? Livvy, come look at this."

I point out the rope and hinges and look up at her face. It reads exactly how I feel. Her hazel eyes expand to wide saucers and one corner of her mouth opens in a surprised and lopsided "O" shape. My face pulls to mimic the look she gives me and my arm juts out for help in standing up.

She grabs my hand and pulls me up to standing. Without another word, we each grab a side of the faceless washing machine barrel and pull. Moving it feels like lifting an unbalanced robot. All the water left inside sloshes around with every single movement, and I can smell my damp clothes begging to be taken out. I can feel sweat beading on my forehead, but when the machine is out of the way and I look up at Livvy, her forehead shows no sign of wear and tear.

I mentally curse her for being in better shape than me, and I make a promise to myself to hit the campus running trail or at least lay off the pastries at Joe's Coffee Shop.

With the sloshy robot off to the side, the rope is there for the taking, ready and waiting to be pulled up, unwrapping whatever is underneath.

"You sure you want to do this? What do you think is under there?" Livvy's breath tickles my hair, she's so close to me. I can feel her nerves scatter in the air.

I shrug my shoulders. "Beats me. You know as much as I do. There's only one way to find out." I wiggle my eyebrows, ready to put the machine project on hold and unlock a mystery right beneath my nose.

Putting my feet on either side of the door, I squat down and wrap my hands around the knotted rope. I'm ready to lift all the weight with my legs, but it lifts surprisingly easily. It's not heavy at all. Just a piece of flooring that had been covered by the stupid broken washing machine.

As I pull it up and back, a musty smell breaks out of the opening. Livvy coughs and gags, as if she had never been to a frat party before. She probably hasn't. But I've been close enough to a frat house to know what they smell like — thank you to frat row on Deuces Street being right in front of my new place — and this smells just like one, with less B.O. and no vomit.

"What is it?" she asks while creeping up to the opening.

I peer around the door I'm holding to look for myself, but I can't quite make out, well, anything. It's dark. No light at all. Which means all the possibilities are under there.

I know all about possibilities. Sometimes they're fantastic surprises that sweep you off your feet. Sometimes, they're creepy men you have to stop in their tracks. You can count on little Mills from the past to know all about that one.

"Let's go in."

I wink at Livvy. She curls up her lip but then shrugs. Her fingers loop through the hair tie kept on her wrist and she uses it to pin up her hair in a loose puff on the top of her head. I have always loved her hair. No matter what she did to it, it always looked like a beautiful sculpture to me, curls forming shapes this way and that. Not like my hair that hangs like flat yellow ribbon by my ears, as if someone ran over it with a steam roller. The best I can do with it is braid it into two blonde tails just to get it out of my face. It works, mostly. That is until some of the strands slither out as if they have a mind of their own.

20

I pull the door open as wide as possible and lay it down on the ground. "Hand me that light," I tell Livvy, pointing to the flashlight I left on the kitchen counter, just in case I needed it to see in the dark depths of that stupid machine. Luckily, we didn't need it for that.

But this? I peer into the depths below. This, we need light for.

The flashlight gives off a bright white light, and when it shines into the darkness beyond the floor, I see there is a set of stairs. Concrete and rough, as if whoever built them there knew they'd need to last a lifetime.

"You ready?" I call behind me, not daring to look away from the abyss in front of my eyes.

"As long as you go first, I'm as ready as I'll ever be." Livvy's voice is as shaky as I feel.

And as I step on the first rung of the stairs, I realize neither of us would ever really be ready for whatever was waiting for us at the last step below.

CHAPTER TWO

Before The Melting Clock House

"This, class, is the only kind of paintbrush I choose to use from now on. I made that decision the moment I first laid my hands on one." Noland lifts up an artisan brush. The handle looks like a polished knobbly stick and the bristles are unlike any I've seen in the typical craft stores. "Luckily, Volga county has a pretty amazing craftsman who has produced a few just for me. Now, I can't promise any of you will have the pleasure of using one of these. It's not like you can find them all willy-nilly wherever, so I need to loan them out sparingly. However, I want to take the rest of our time together today to show you how to care for a *real* brush like this, because I'm sure a few of you will have the pleasure of creating a masterpiece with one." Noland gives the class a wink. I like to think that maybe it's meant for me.

Everyone calls him Noland because that's what he prefers. Day one of every class, he demands his students to drop the titles "professor" and "doctor" because they sound too snobby. He wants to be an equal to his students, learning as much from us as we do from him.

"Most paintbrushes you'll find on the store shelves are cheap, made of polyester or nylon. After a few uses, they splay out in all directions, like an old toothbrush." He flicks the bristles of the one he's holding back and forth. They move like water. Well, as much like water as a solid can be, I guess.

You know the kind of professors who pat themselves on the back by basing a lesson on a book they wrote, a podcast they hosted, or some obscure TV show they appeared on ten years ago? Noland is the opposite. He's basing this lesson on someone else's handiwork. Craftsmanship like that isn't just mass-produced and sold in stores like Craft Your Pants.

Yup. We actually have a craft store named Craft Your Pants right down 42nd street, or Deuces, as most people call it.

And, yeah, we actually do call it Deuces. Partially because it's Forty-second Street. And partially because it's also the street where all the frat houses are lined up. If you walk down the row of houses in the dark, you need to pay extra attention to where you're stepping. You might just land a foot in someone else's deuce. Apparently, the bathroom lines in those houses are always too long to wait in if you have to take a dump.

Frat boys are gross. And stupid. Don't forget stupid.

"Miss Ellis, do you know?"

Crap. Called on.

"Do I know…" I let it dangle because Noland will always fill in the gaps.

"Do you know the best way to wash these particular brushes?"

Oh, duh. "Yeah. Mild soap and warm water. Always does the trick!"

He lets out a loud buzzing noise, and chuckles ripple throughout the room. "Sorry, Mills, that's incorrect." He gives me a wink anyway. Noland always knows how to make you feel better when you answer wrong.

"Didn't you say there was some kind of special oil to use?" Kyle, a showoff meathead in the back of the class, answers. "You, like, mentioned it last week, right?" Kyle is also one of those gross frat brothers. I'm pretty sure I dodged one of his deuces once or twice before.

"Castor oil!" Malory calls out after him.

She's one of those girls who only get confidence after someone else speaks up. She also happens to be one of the freshmen who snuck her

23

way into an advanced art class. Not sure how she did it, but I have mad respect for her for it.

Kyle laughs under his breath. "I'm pretty sure my grandmother uses that to help her poop."

I'm pretty sure Fratboy Kyle has taken his grandmother's advice once or twice judging by the consistency of poop I've almost stepped in down Deuces.

The class lets out a laugh again, and Noland combs his hands through his hair. "Alright, alright. Yes; some people do use castor oil as a laxative. You can also use it as an antifungal or acne treatment."

"Something else Kyle could use," Sam pipes up in the back of the class.

I like Sam. She's punchy once in a while, which you'd never expect from a girl who always wore pearl earrings. And she speaks the truth. Kyle does have a face full of breakouts, usually whenever he's off-again with his on-again-off-again girlfriend, Janelle.

Noland lifts his hand to quiet another round of laughter from the class. "But in this room, we're going to use it to clean our brushes." He strokes the knobbly wooden handle of the one he's holding. "Of course, if you choose to use the cheap nylon brushes instead, I'm not going to stop you. In fact, some of you are going to just have to deal with them." He lifts his eyes to address the whole class, and I swear his eyes land on mine. "But if you are lucky enough to use the *good* brushes, then you're going to need to clean them properly. Take care of them as if they were precious babies of your own."

"Wahhhh," Kyle fake cries from his seat.

"Of course, Mr. Warren can go ahead and use the crappy brushes. He can't seem to take care of his own needs, let alone the precious baby of someone else's."

This time, Noland lets the class play out their laughter while Kyle tries to hide his embarrassment.

But me? I'm concentrating on Noland and what he's doing behind his desk. Because if these weird knobbly brushes are the best of the best, then these are the brushes I am going to use. I'll beg and plead to use them if needed. I know not everyone takes art seriously, but I want to do everything I can to perfect mine. There's not a whole lot in this world I'm great at, but I know my art is good. Perhaps by learning with the right tools, I'll be great.

He opens a drawer and pulls out... a bunsen burner? What the heck? This isn't science class. I'll have to ask Livvy to see if there is any missing equipment in the science lab. Sneaking away with a burner seems like something Noland would do, if it were for the benefit of his art students. Livvy's my best friend, by the way. And she's a science nerd. She would probably be able to explain everything Noland is doing right now before he even does it.

As he plugs the burner in, the class's laughter dies down a little more. He starts it up and the laughter is gone. Fire makes things serious.

He pulls open another drawer. Inside is a jar full of beans.

Beans. That takes a moment for my brain to register.

He places them in a glass bowl above the fire and lets it heat up.

"Of course, you could buy castor oil at any supermarket or grocery store. But honestly? Homemade is always best." Noland looks up at the class and runs his hands through his hair. "Now I know a bunch of college kids aren't going to go off and make their own oils at home, so I'll have plenty to use in the studio here. However," and he taps the bowl above the flame, "I still want to show you how to nurture your art in the best ways possible. I'm sure some of you will take the initiative to do that on your own." I get another wink from him. He's right, though. I'll be sure to treat my brushes with absolute respect. Especially if it's one of these.

"Once these beans heat up a little, they'll be ready to blend into a paste. Unfortunately, Volga campus doesn't give me enough time to sit here and wait for beans to boil, so I'll show you what that paste looks like."

Noland reaches back into the drawer he got the beans out of and shows us another jar. This one is full of golden paste. He shrugs as he holds it up. "From there, you just strain and store." A third jar shows a liquid oil. It slowly sloshes around the inside like a lazy little wave. "When you get to this point, you know you've got liquid gold."

"Can you, like, sell it on the black market, then?" Kyle's attempt at a joke falls flat.

Noland's face does, too.

"No, Mr. Warren. The black market doesn't want your homemade laxative." He holds the jar up so the fluorescent lights shine through the glass. "However, this is worth its weight and more in the art world. At least when you're using the right kind of brushes."

He unscrews the top of the jar and dips the tip of the brush into it. Then, he stops. He pauses for dramatic effect and looks up at the class. Malory giggles, and he gives her a wink. He's really giving them out today. Then, he juts the rest of the bristles in and opens his mouth in an "O" shape, which typically indicates that he's pretty proud of what he's done. This time, I think Noland is assuming we all "get" it. I'm not sure I do.

"You see, castor oil is a natural moisturizer."

Good thing he's about to clue me in.

"And after several uses, your brushes dry out. They become brittle and weak." He sloshes it around a little in the oil. "Which means your paints will end up splattered all over the place instead of gliding along your canvas like...like-"

"Like your feet on a wet bathroom floor?" Kyle chimes in.

Noland nods. "Yeah. I guess so. But less...gross."

The clock on the wall chimes 10:00 — the signal that class is over. Everyone stands up, and the sound of metal chair legs scraping against the floor fills the room, but even though all my classmates are making their way out of the classroom, I stay rooted in my seat, mesmerized by the way this crazy-looking brush is floating its bristles in the oil in front of me.

They're swimming inside, like a kaleidoscope. Any chips of paint that had been on them have slipped off and are floating around like little specs of colorful dirt and grime.

"Class has ended, Ms. Mills." Noland breaks me out of my stare.

"I know." As I ease out of my chair and pull my bag over my shoulder, I take another look at the bristles. They really don't look like anything I have ever seen before. "It's just, I'm curious." I flip my skateboard that had been resting against my desk into my hand with my foot. "Does the oil do anything for regular brushes? Like the kind you can grab from any 'ol store?"

He taps the handle of the brush on the side of the jar. Then, Noland pulls out a rag from his pocket and wipes the bristles clean.

"The brushes from the store are... how should I say this? They're inferior. Sure, you could use them if you really wanted to, but I'm not sure why anyone would when you could use something that will really unlock your talent." Noland runs the bristles within the rag again and examines them. "So, sure, you could use castor oil to clean off and moisturize a regular, cheap brush, but it would be like cleaning off a toilet brush with specialty soap when you should really throw it in the trash and get something better."

I nod. I think I understand. "So, you're saying if you want to do something right, you need to use the right tools?" A heavy weight sits in my chest. I don't know if I'll be lucky enough to actually use one of these special brushes this semester. And if I can't use the *right* tools, what would that mean for my grade? My art?

Satisfied the brush is now clean, he holds it up to the light. "Bingo," he tells me. Then, he holds out the brush with his hand. That weight in my chest lightens and a little bit of weightless hope settles in its place.

"For me?" I'm unsure if he means it or if I'm reading his motions wrong. I hope I'm not.

"Of course, Ms. Ellis."

I take a few steps forward to his desk and use my free hand to accept this gift. "But… why?" I have no idea why Noland has given me something that should be saved for someone special. Not everyone will get a chance to use this, and yet, he's choosing me?

"Because I know you have talent to unlock. I've seen what you've produced before. It's my favorite work in my office."

My face grows hot. I know he likes to display student artwork on his office shelves, but I didn't think he had a favorite.

"But shouldn't the rest of the class also get to use this?"

He shrugs. "Not everyone will take care of it nearly as carefully as I know you will. And there will be more, eventually. But this one." He points to the knobbly handle in my hand. "This one I think was meant for you. Go ahead and use it. You'll see what I mean."

I nod. I get it. Well, not really. But I understand that he believes this brush was built for me. So I'll take it back to my dorm room and see what I can create. I know it'll be something good. Something important.

My skateboard hits the floor, and I shove the brush into my pocket. "I'll be sure to use it, Noland!"

And with that, I'm out of the classroom, in the hall, and right on the campus sidewalk. Whatever is special about this paintbrush, I'm going to find out.

CHAPTER THREE

Joe's Coffee is filled to the brim, every seat taken up by the butts of college students and professors who would rather spend seven dollars on magic bean water than a dollar for on-campus sludge.

Seriously, the student union coffee is gross. And no one seems to actually get a jolt of energy while drinking it. Instead, they get indigestion. How are we supposed to study on a stomach full of acid? Nope. Joe's is about the only coffee the small town of Volga has to offer. That's why whenever I have a break in classes, I make sure to roll myself on down there and save Livvy a seat. It's my second home, away from the dorms. And it smells better, too. Besides, the caffeine from this place is probably the only thing keeping my body running some days.

"Hey, girl." Livvy helps herself to the seat across from me, squeezing her elbows on the little room left on the tiny round table.

"Hey, Livvy. Another fun day in the world of sciency genius?"

"Meh." She blows the steam off the top of the oversized mug in her hands. "We're not exactly mixing up potions or blowing things up. It's a lot of calculations." She squints her eyes and rubs her temple. A tiny section of baby hairs slips away from its carefully gelled place. "How about you?"

"It's all paintbrushes today."

"Paint brushes?" She's not impressed. I don't blame her. It doesn't exactly sound exciting.

"Paintbrushes." I nod. "Noland taught us how to clean paintbrushes." My tone comes out snarky and deadpan through my curled upper lip, but then I take another sip of black coffee and uncurl it. "It was actually kind of cool, though. Nothing like I've seen before." I pull the one

Noland gave me out of my back pocket and marvel at its shape some more.

Livvy takes the handle in her fingers and spins it a few times, watching the bristles shimmy with the motion. "Looks like a regular paintbrush to me. But if you're looking for more like it, I bet Stark knows where to find more of its kind."

Remember how I said we had an art store called Craft Your Pants? Stark works there. Has since he graduated high school. I suppose Volga townies never really grow out of the area.

"He did *what* now?" a nearby voice pipes up and breaks both my and Livvy's focus on the brush.

"Shh, don't let the whole world know," a second pipes up.

It's Malory from class, and a tall blonde sorority girl I always see around but can never remember her name. They're at a table next to us, and with their *hushed-yelling* voices, I force my eyes straight ahead at Livvy even though my ears are fine-tuning themselves to the conversation.

Livvy's eyes are also latched onto mine.

"I mean, it's not so terrible, is it? It's just bodies," Malory yell-whispers.

And now I really don't want my ears to be so damn good at picking up conversation. But they're doing it anyway. And my brain can't order them to stop. Livvy's wide eyes tell me that her ears are doing the same, and she also wants to force her ears to shut.

"I guess a little bit of body play can be fun?" the blonde yell-whispers back.

And holy crap now that seemed to escalate quickly.

Livvy's dark eyes widen more, and I can see her jaw clench tight.

Through my peripheral vision, I see Malory shrug her shoulders. "I don't really know what I'm doing, but he's teaching me what to do." Then she pauses and I hear her grumble, "Oh, my stomach hurts."

Her response is just like mine. I feel queasy. My jaw clenches, too. Her tone is uncomfortable, she's not exactly shouting this news from the rooftops, and here's this other blonde, dressed in the standard Alpha pink shirt who's literally laughing at this poor girl and whatever happened between her body and this other guy's.

I had my fair share of boys who eyed me up and down on Volga's campus. But I ended those stares with crossed arms and spitting on the ground. If they persisted, my fist would somehow find its way in their stomach, and I'd use my skateboard to get the heck outta there. I didn't come to college to get swooped up by some guy who wanted to pick me up for the weekend and dump me like last Tuesday's leftovers.

I've seen what that does to people.

That's not my style. And it shouldn't be anyone else's.

Especially the Freshmen girls who are the literal babies on campus.

"Was he at least a... gentleman about it?" The blonde's interest is piqued and I can't believe she wants to know the details about Malory's body and whoever else's.

"Mariëtte!" Malory scoffs. And then she offers another pained, "My stomach..."

Across from me, Livvy snickers into her cup of coffee.

"Well, you know big sisters have to look after their littles and all that." That was sorority talk right there. It always makes me uncomfortable how the Greeks talk about themselves as if they're one big happy family while color-coding their wardrobe with matching t-shirts and jumpers.

"It's not like that..." Malory is no longer yell-whispering. She's whisper-whispering. Yet, my stupid ears are still dialed into her voice like it's a radio station meant just for me. "It's just. Well, I kind of had to put on a brave face, you know?"

Had. To.

Bile is rising in my throat and I have to chug piping hot bean water to keep it from ricocheting out of my mouth.

"Hello, ladies."

And now the bean water tastes like bile because of course the only thing more disgusting than this conversation is Professor Crane himself, the college equivalent of your least favorite PE teacher, who is now hovering over Malory and Mariëtte.

Livvy's brows knit together and, in an effort to drown out whatever the heck is going on over the table, she says, "It just looks like a regular paintbrush to me."

I nod because I'm not really listening to her. I'm listening to Crane's greasy voice slide all over the conversation next door.

"Have you been working on what I showed you?"

"You've been practicing real hard for me, haven't you?"

I hate the taste of bile, and it's getting stronger with every syllable he oozes out.

"Mills," Livvy's voice is in the back of my ears but it's being shadowed out by Greasy Gross oily Crane.

"Next time, you'll have to show me what your body can do after our lessons."

Holy grossness, Batman, what is this man saying?

"Mills!" Livvy's voice actively snaps me out of the Crane-daze. "I said do you know where he got this?" She flicks my brush back and forth between her fingers.

I shrug and put my large coffee cup to my mouth. It's empty. Damn. "I don't know. But it's definitely unique, isn't it?" I wish there was something that could wash the verbal sewage I just heard out of my ears.

Livvy hands the brush over and I slip it back into my pocket. "Like I said, it looks like a regular brush to me. Just with a fancier handle. But again, I'm pretty sure Stark would be able to nail down where it came from if you ask him." She gives me a sly smile, the same one that always urges me to go visit her brother to exchange awkward talk and blushing cheeks.

She thinks we'd make a good couple.

I think she's dreaming.

My cup dings as it hits back on the table. The seats next to us are now filled with a couple of frat boys who are wearing matching backward baseball caps and punching each other in the arms. Malory and Mariëtte are gone. And so is Greasy Crane. But their innuendo conversation still lingers in my ears.

"Didn't you hear that?"

Livvy hangs her head. I know she doesn't really want to discuss it. Not here anyway. That's someone else's business, and she doesn't want to stick her nose in someone else's dirty laundry. But there isn't a strong enough q-tip that could ever clean my ears out of the words Crane said.

"Didn't that sound like..."

"We don't know anything about that," she cuts me off.

"But you heard it, too, didn't you?"

She pulls her eyes up to meet mine again, and I notice again how her curls are struggling to stay in place. She did have a hard day in the science lab. She just didn't want to tell me about it earlier.

"I know what you heard. I heard it, too. But as creepy as it is, there's no proof of anything. And you can't just knock on Professor Crane's office door and demand to know if he's sleeping with students, can you?"

So she did come to the same conclusion I did. She's just not wanting to claim it as truth.

As I shift in my seat, the paintbrush rolls in my pocket. No. If I were to ask him outright if he was doing something sleazy and gross, he's sure to brush me off. Give me some lame excuse. But maybe — I touch my back pocket — maybe I can put my tool and talent to work.

33

"Livvy, can I come to your dorm room later? I have an idea."

Even though she rolls her eyes, I know the answer. Her room is always less crowded than mine. Plus, it makes it so much easier to work when I have her by my side. Livvy is a better muse than my actual roommate. I smile and thank her for it. She'll let me over, as long as her roommate, Janelle, isn't there. And I'll have my way with the biggest canvas I can get my hands on.

***

The shelves at Craft Your Pants are made for visually stimulated college students. They're color-coded based on the supplies they carry. Green shelves for fabric. Orange for yarn. And brown is for paint.

Why they chose brown for the most colorful medium possible, I'll never know. But, it reminded me of Deuces, which always makes me want to fill my basket as quickly as possible, and check out at the register just as fast.

In go the blues and greens, shades of tans and black. A greasy black. The kind that looks like the way Crane's voice sounds. I scootch over to the brushes and pick them over. Nope. They're all crappy nylon and polyester. Inferior. None of them look like the one I have stashed in my back pocket.

Humph.

I head over to the next section in the aisle. Canvases. The world of possibility on a rectangle. Hm. The typical sixteen by twenties won't do. I'll need something bigger. Something that will make a point.

There she is. A seventy-two by thirty-six inch stretched canvas, just begging me to bring her home and help tell a story. I'm sure the recurring customer credit I've accumulated will cover most of the cost. With one arm crooked in the basket handle and the other awkwardly balancing the biggest possible canvas over my head, I make my way to the register. I bump into a lady down the next aisle and, judging by the sound of rattling items on the floor, I may have knocked something out of her hands. Or, a lot of some*things*.

I cringe, apologize, and continue on my mission.

Stark is waiting for me at the register, just as he always is, and when he greets me, my face grows hot. Looking into his face is like looking at Livvy. They have the same dark skin. The same short curly hair.

Except, his jawline is a little more angular.

And his eyes are just a teensy bit wider.

And that dimple is just enough for my stomach to flip and flop.

"Hey, Mills. Planning something big, I see."

I bite my lip and tell my heated face to cool down. "You have no idea."

"I imagine not. Sis always says you never do anything too small. Go big or go home, right?"

I flip the canvas around so the barcode is easy for him to scan. "I guess in this case, it's go big and go home."

He chuckles, and it feels good to make my friend's big brother laugh. It always makes whatever nerves I have wash away with ease.

"Say, Stark, I've got a question for ya."

He leans over the counter, and I can smell eagerness on him. I suppose when you've memorized everyone in the same small town, it's easy to get excited over other people's chit-chat.

Balancing the canvas on the floor, I reach into my back pocket and weasel out the brush that's been hiding there. "Do you happen to have anything like this in stock? Or know anything about it?"

Stark's hand brushes up against mine as he takes the handle from me. He pulls it close to his face and turns it back and forth. His eyes squint, taking in the knobbly details of the handle. The bristles fan out and collect back together when he circles a fingertip on them.

After thorough speculation, Stark hands it back to me and shrugs his shoulders. "Nothing like that comes off our trucks. This definitely looks like it's handmade by someone who knows what they're doing. But I tell you what," he side-smiles, "I'll keep my eyes open and ask around. We get all kinds of people coming in and out of here. I'm bound to come across someone who crafts their own tools."

"Thanks, Stark. I kinda thought you might not have them in store. I appreciate you looking out."

"Will you kids quit your yapping already?" The woman with coke-bottle glasses joins the line. Well, she stands behind me, forming a line of one, anyway. And I can hear the spittle fly from her teeth at every word.

I choke down a gag, pretending my ears weren't just violated by that.

"Sorry, lady," I say, and I shove my paintbrush back into my pocket to free one hand up for a bag of paints and the other for my canvas.

"Darn right you're sorry! Kids these days don't have any respect. Just think they can eat up everyone else's time."

I want to tell her that if she's so bothered by so many "darned kids" maybe she shouldn't live in a college town where those exact same darned kids are going to end up shopping in the same darned shops as her.

But I know better. She and her momma and her momma's momma have probably lived in Volga since before campus was much of a campus at all. There's no talking those kinds of people out of a place where they originated. It's just best to nod, smile, and move on your merry way, hoping the next time you run into them, you just get lumped into their general annoyances rather than distinctly remembering you, doubling their irritation. It's always hard to tell what kind of crazy thing will happen when an irritated townie has burned your face into memory.

I give her my best smile and look back at Stark. His kind eyes apologize. Don't know why he'd be sorry. He's not the one spitting out words three feet in front of me.

"Thanks," I tell him as he hands me a receipt and a bright yellow paper. At the top, it says, **Fine Arts Festival. Sponsored by: Memento Mori Society**. I don't know who or what Memento Mori Society is, but I do know the festival. It happens every year. I shove them both into my other back pocket to balance myself out.

"Be sure to look at that later, Mills. The flyer, that is. From what Livvy says and what I believe, I think you'd be a good fit."

"Good fit?"

"For the fine arts festival."

This year, it's supposed to be big. Like, big big. And that's really saying something. Usually, it fills up with talented people who come out of the woodwork. Names no one has heard of and faces that have never been seen. They show off a handful of paintings and people from all the big towns around Volga come to see, browse, and shop with wads of cash in their pockets.

I like that Stark believes I'd fit in there. Even though I'm not sure he's actually seen anything I've done before. But the thought of his approval makes me nervous. Would I really be a good fit? Next to all the amazing artists bound to be there?

The coke-bottle glasses lady huffs again, but the way Stark is smiling at me, I'm pretty sure she can hold on for just a split second more.

"I ain't got time for you kids to make googly eyes at each other. Some people have things to do, plans to make, and circles to get back to."

Circles to get back to. That's a weird way to say that she has a planned bingo event or cribbage match or whatever it is nearly blind old women who spit do.

I shrug her off, give Stark a wave, and gather my supplies the best I can. I find my skateboard where I left it: by the shop's front door. With a foot, I kick it to the floor, swing the bag to the crook of my elbow, balance the canvas on my head, and skate out. The lady huffs and spits again, but I ain't got time for whatever that's about. I have a canvas to paint. And a point to make.

CHAPTER FOUR

Malory

Malory Gibbons buckles under the weight of pain in her abdomen. There has been a growth in stomach cramps and she can't quite figure out why. Everything in her mental checklist has cleared.

Bad dining hall food? No. She has steered clear of anything that's been left out on the salad bar and took extra responsibility in checking how fresh each hot plate is.

Nerves? No. Exams are still weeks away, and even if there is a pop quiz, she is pretty sure she'd ace it. Excelling in classes is her specialty.

Menstrual cramps? No; her period finished the week before last.

This is different from any typical pains she's experienced before. This feels like —

Ughhhh!

It feels like death.

"Agghhh!"

She screams out in agony, clutching her midsection, mentally willing this feeling to go. Or even to lessen. She'd gladly take on the worst menstrual cramps and the flu at the same time if it meant she wouldn't have to feel this awful gut-twisting sensation anymore.

And within a few seconds, the pain dissipates enough so that she can stand straight and take a step. Relief. Sweet, sweet relief.

Okay, Malory. Take a step.

Her foot moves forward on the pavement.

Take another step.

She can smell the freshly cut grass in the common area.

And another.

She fills her lungs with the night air

Fresh air is good. Fresh air will help.

That's what she had told herself before leaving her dorm, and that's what she continues to tell herself now. Fresh air always helps.

Except not right now, it doesn't.

"Ahhh!" Malory screams out in agony again.

Why is no one around? Why is no one out on campus?

She reminds herself that it's eleven o'clock at night. The buses into town finished running for the day. And since it is still midweek, the frats are still planning for their Thirsty Thursday parties. Even Deuces felt empty, quiet, dead.

There is no reason to be out unless someone is bored enough for a late-night stroll. Had she not needed to get out of bed in an attempt to walk off this feeling, she wouldn't be out here either. But writhing in her bunk bed wasn't helping her at all, so she had left her campus dorm hoping to walk it out.

"Walk it out, champ." Isn't that what he had told her? *"Walk it out. Ease your muscles. Calm your nerves. Walk it out. Walk it out. Walk it out."*

Her stomach fills with acid. It crawls up her intestines, clasps around her heart, and squeezes tight. It burns her from the inside out. She swears she can feel it making sour holes to leak out to the outside world.

And then the acid climbs from its posts inside her stomach, intestines, and heart, and up up up into her throat where it worms its way into her mouth.

"Ahhhh!"

She's on the pavement, in a pile of vomit, and she can't get herself to stand up straight. Here, on the ground, her mouth gapes open. It's like it's melting into an open shape she can't close shut. She closes her eyes, but even there, she can't block out the sickness. Behind her eyelids, she

40

sees liquidy oranges and yellows. Swirls of macabre rottenness that pulls her entire being down down down and away from reality.

She tries to scream, wants to scream, aims to scream. She is *The Scream*.

The painting that drips into a permanent horror.

"What is happening?" she whisper-cries out into the open, hoping a bored student with attentive ears will hear her, and offer up a helping hand, a cup of water, or at least a napkin for her chin.

But no one is there.

No one can help.

No one is around to even know she's crippled in soured pain, screaming even when she can't scream.

"Malory?"

The single sweet word breaks through the darkness, and she can feel the warmth coming straight from its syllables. The sourness eases, just a little.

She nods. Yes. Malory. That is her name. Whoever has found her knows her. Which means they are even more helpful than a random bored student. This is the knight in shining armor she needed. The attentive person who could wipe her chin and carry her to safety.

"Malory? Here." A hand reaches out in front of her. Even in the darkness, she knows its familiar shape. It has held her before, protected her. It's been there to warm her sides, pull her in, and tell her how talented she is.

It has also touched her when she said no.

And then it touched her again to make her say yes.

But however many times she said no and yes, and yes and no to that hand didn't matter. It is here now, offering help. If she could scream "yes" she would scream it from the rooftops.

She eases her hand into his. Painfully, she puts weight back onto her feet. She stands as straight as she can as the images of oranges and

41

yellows swirl to the back of her mind. They could stay there, away from the surface. They could go to a place that can't engulf her everything.

His eyes look so concerned, like he can't comprehend what he is seeing in front of him. As if he could see the same swirls and shapes on the outside that she felt under the surface. She doesn't blame him. She must look like a wounded animal, desperate to be put under and out of its misery. His eyes. They take her in, drinking in her hurt. She can almost feel her pain dissolve into them. If he is going to absorb the orange and yellow sickness for himself, she'll let him.

"Here, let me help you."

He scoops her up into his arms — A real knight in shining armor. He strode in through the darkness of the night to find her, *to find her*, and take her to safety in his arms.

Saying yes was good. It's what she had to do before, so she could say yes to him now. It makes swimming sense in her lightening head.

Walking. He is walking now. She can feel his movement, one foot gaining traction and then another. Where is he taking her?

Does it matter? No. She doesn't have to carry her own weight anymore. That's what matters. She doesn't have to make the effort; she doesn't have it in her muscles anymore to try. She doesn't have to fight against the face of screaming agony.

"That's it," she hears him croon. His voice sounds like water. It floats in and out and around her and she is now swimming in it, the same way his eyes swam in her and the sour taste swam within her.

Everything is an ocean of hurt and fatigue and fading hope, and where is he taking her?

The ground is cold and hard. It's still dark and it's still so cold. They're still outside.

Is he still here?

"There, there."

He is. Thank goodness.

A hand cradles the top of her head. It spider-grips around the bun she always wears, and within a moment, her hair falls to the side.

"What? Why did you…?"

It smells where she is, but she can't tell if it's something around her or if the smell is coming from herself.

"There, there."

It's too hard for her to ask more, so she doesn't. She feels her head droop and her insides burn. She has now melted into the image of *The Scream.*

The last thing she hears is a snipping sound, like scissors cutting through string. More hair droops into her face and everything goes dark.

CHAPTER FIVE

"Ugh! I can't believe him!" Janelle, Livvy's roommate, busts into the dorm room right in the middle of a paint stroke.

She's freaking lucky I have steady hands. The burnt orange paint slides across the canvas exactly where I want it to, despite her rude interruption. I should have seen this coming. Janelle and Kyle are *that* couple. Always in a perpetual cycle from romantic Hell.

"Sounds like it's time for a woo-sahhh," Livvy exhales. "Tea, Janelle?" She holds up a canister of camomile, and I chuckle under my breath. I've seen the way this girl throws a hissy fit. It's going to take a lot more than a cup of tea to calm those nerves down.

Janelle growls. She freaking *growls* like a rabid animal and throws herself onto her bed. Guess I was right. It's off-again time with Kyle. He's going to need some of Noland's caster oil for his skin.

I dip my brush into a glob of brown paint, impressed by how the bristles take it. I'm going to do my best to ignore whatever drama is about to unfold here, because that's not the kind of drama worth participating in.

All that matters is the canvas in front of me and the way the picture comes to life. I don't even have to think of it much. There's no real planning or strict guidelines I'm putting on it. I just steadily breathe and let the painting happen on its own. Then I breathe out, letting my heart tell my hands the message it needs to take.

That's what art is: the perfect marriage of an artist's intent and the message beating life onto the canvas itself.

Janelle muffles a yell into her pillow, infiltrating my process just enough for me to pause before I move the brush again. Her off-white t-shirt crinkles as her muscles contract while she screams. On the other side of the room, Livvy picks up her own cup of tea she made before Janelle busted through the room like a five-year-old forced to eat broccoli.

"Woo-sahhh," she exhales again and takes a sip. She gestures to the canvas I'm working on. "Think she'll help give you a muse?" Livvy asks under her breath.

"Not unless she's also been pulled into Crane's office for some *extracurricular activity*," I hiss back. But my gut tells me Crane isn't the "him" Janelle is talking about. So no, she's not going to serve as any kind of muse for this painting.

"He's so insufferable!" Janelle wails out as she punches her pillow in rapid machine-gun succession. She grunts again and throws the pillow against the wall, then stuffs the corner into her mouth and bites.

I don't think she understands what the word insufferable means.

"Girl, I think your neurons are on fire. Time to calm them down so you can figure out whatever…whatever this is." Livvy waves her hand in Janelle's direction indicating all the baggage she just carried into the room.

"He's been sleeping with her, I just know it!"

"Woo-sahhh," Livvy's voice is a little louder now, trying to demand the calm Janelle's way.

But by the way Janelle is still tearing away at her pillow like a chihuahua in a fight, I know this show isn't going to end unless we at least play along a little. "I'm assuming you're talking about Kyle?" My grip tightens on my brush, knowing at the sound of his name, Janelle's nerves are probably going to spike again.

"Who else would I be talking about, moron?" Yup. That's the kind of response I expected.

"And who exactly is he sleeping with?" I dip my silken brush bristles back into my paint and let Janelle's anger fuel mine so I can get this just right.

"I don't know. Some *girl*." Her voice whines out the last word as if saying the single syllable makes her sick. "And I tell you what, if I see her anywhere near him again, I'm going to cut off her head and throw it in the river."

Well, that escalated quickly. And with the small campus this is, whoever *she* is, the chances of her getting anywhere close to either Janelle or Kyle is... well, it's just bound to happen.

"And how do you know he's sleeping with her?"

"Girl, you better be careful with those questions," Livvy tells me through her teeth.

"How? HOW?"

Janelle is spitting bullets of anger out of her mouth and they shoot directly into my chest, run down my arm, and force my hand to move in fast strokes. Left. Right. Up. Down. Crisscross and around the corner. Splatters of orange and yellow and brown and blue are all over the place. The oddly familiar color pallet begs me for more.

"What... what is that?" Somewhere within Janelle, a switch flips and her voice is different. Even though her face is still red and there's a pillow feather stuck to the side of her mouth, she's almost calm, curious.

"What, this?" My brushstrokes stop, and I spin my brush around. The crooked handle points to the wet paint on my canvas. "This is just a little project of mine."

"That's boobs," she says.

I frown. She's not wrong. It is. Sure enough, right in front of me is a set of breasts. Perky enough to be jealous of. But it's also not just boobs. "It's a statement. It's art." But I don't expect her to understand. How could she?

"No. That's boobs."

Nope; a preppy girl full of high emotions really isn't going to get it. And I'm not going to try to explain it when she's talking about ripping off some girl's head to throw it in the river, so I nod and agree with her.

"Yes, Janelle. That's boobs. And those..." I point to another figure in the painting. One that's got a hooked nose and greasy hair. "...are dangly bits." I spin the brush around in my hand again and get back to work. If nothing else, the shock value alone will speak volumes when I display it.

CHAPTER SIX

Andrea

Music thumps through Andrea Shepherd's body, shaking her organs up, down, left, right, and within the rhythm of everyone dancing around her. Thirsty Thursdays were the best times to sneak into the frat house parties as a townie girl who never had the spare change to attend college.

Not that Andrea needs to do any sneaking. She fits right in. She looks the part of a college girl and learned to sound the part, too. If she ended every sentence in an upward sound as if she was full of questions and no answers, she could get away with anything in one of these houses. And if she threw on a pale pink shirt, she could easily pass as one of the "sisters" that floats around, getting drunk off of whatever the boys poured in their cups.

So every Thursday, this is where she was. Rain or shine, she'd choose a house at random and help herself in. No one ever knew she was pretending to be anything she wasn't. They'd treat her just like everyone else through those doors: a girl with plenty of future ahead of her and a night she needed to forget.

Tonight is no different. She needs to be away from her dilapidated house and deadbeat boyfriend. She swears one day she'll leave him, when he would become too much to handle. For now, the bruises on her arm are easy enough to cover. And Thursday parties are the exact getaway she needs.

Music. Drinks. Food. Drinks. Boys. Drinks.

It is all a tornado that would whisk her up and spit her out with the temporary memory loss of whatever she's trying to forget.

It is beautiful.

Andrea wipes her hands on her oversized shawl, the one she made herself with scrapes of cotton and fabric markers. Whenever she wears it, she always feels like a powerhouse. Like she has some kind of ability to control her place in the world. This is her talent. This is proof of her creativity. Wearing it gives her the extra confidence to be whoever she needs to be until she has to wobble her way back to the life she's trying to escape from.

She grabs a cup off the table in front of her. It's hers. Or, at least she thinks it's hers. Either way, it's a drink worth drinking. She tips it back and feels the jungle juice warm her throat.

Cup in hand, she walks to the beat thumping through the walls and into her organs. She'd peruse, search out someone to spend an hour with. Someone to dance with. Someone to share the sugary taste of jungle juice with so they could drown themselves in a blur of alcohol together.

A guy with a square jaw is standing by a keg. He's cute enough, if it weren't for the fact that his mouth hangs open like a fish every time he responds to someone's question. Girls are lined up with their cups in hand, each of them wearing a crop top and shorts no longer than Andrea's underwear. She looks down at her own clothes. Fully covered. And with stains on her jeans. She should have at least tried to look for something clean in her closet.

Then she looks at the crowd around her. No; she shouldn't have. She could have been wearing a paper bag and not a single one of these people would have given her any notice. They are all busy trying to impress each other. They don't have any time to give to the poor townie girl who barely exists.

She stands in line behind a girl with pin straight curves and a voice that sounds like mud. Every word slurs into the next in thick syllables, making it impossible to comprehend if she is even speaking the English language.

"I wwwaaaa- noooot-errr."

Andrea rolls her eyes. No one should be filling this girl's cup up. She sounds too far gone.

Andrea looks down at her own empty cup and reminds herself of her own hunger for more. Then again, maybe this girl wants to drink away her days of abuse and hardship just like Andrea does. If that's the case, who is she to judge?

Drink away, stick girl.

As the line inches up, Andrea can see the square-jawed guy flirt with each of the girls. His eyes narrow, his mouth hangs open just a little too much, and his hand grazes their sides. It's a ticket. An unspoken payment for a full cup.

Finally, the slurry-girl reaches the front of the line. Wobbling, she hands over her cup. A little of what's left sloshes at the bottom. "Oh! I fooooo-gotsome." She tips it back, tapping the bottom to make sure every last drop lands in her mouth. All the more room for more.

"Aaaa-dun!" She hiccups, then tosses the cup back in front of her.

A lazy smile creeps along the square-jaw guy's mouth. His hands reach out to graze her side. No, not graze. He full-on grabs at it, pulls her toward him, and forces the girl to land stradled in his lap. Within seconds, they're entangled with each other, mouths glued together like magnets trying to find their way to the right poles.

Andrea squeezes by them, grabs the keg's nozzle, and fills her own cup. It's not like she has the currency to get by this guy anyway. The girl who was in front of her stumbles, squeals, and one of her arms hits Andrea's cup.

If this girl were in her right mind, Andrea would thank her for paying the toll for both of them.

With a full cup in hand, she weaves in and out of the crowded house. It seems like everyone is either already paired up or already passed out. Andrea is alone in her quest to erase her day.

Fine by me.

She tosses her cup up and chugs back the cheap beer inside. Maybe tonight is a bust. Maybe she should get one more drink to go and walk herself home. Maybe her boyfriend would be passed out by now and she could escape the rest of the night through sleep.

Back to the kitchen she goes to slosh a ladle full of jungle juice back into the cup and drink-walk her way out the front door.

The night air hits her skin. Cool. Calm. It's a lot quieter outside, which means her thoughts grow a lot louder to compensate.

He's got to be home by now. He's going to be waiting for me. That's how it was last time and I still have the bruises to show for it. I don't want to see him. I have nowhere to go. I have no one to go with. I can't be on the streets. I can't do that to myself. Not again...

Looking up, the stars dance in the sky. They circle around each other, with little light trails behind them. Whatever mixture she forced in her stomach is probably making her eyes dance, but it feels better to think that the stars are doing it on their own. They are running from their spots, like she did every Thursday, only to come back to the same place, unhappy and unsettled.

"Hey," a voice stops her thoughts from running any further. "You look like you have the weight of the world on your shoulders."

Andrea nods. She does feel the entire weight of the world on her shoulders. But how does this man know? How could he even see? She can't even see his face from where she is. He is just a moving outline in the dark.

51

Tentatively, she wobbles a step forward in the direction the man's voice came from. He's leaning against a fence post, the lid of a baseball cap pointed down to cover his face in shadow.

"Why aren't you inside?" she asks. She wants to know what makes this astute man want to separate himself from the rest of the crowd. Why he would be standing alone in the dark, watching the stars circle the sky as well?

"I could ask you the same." He lifts his chin, and the baseball cap no longer hides his entire features. He looks mature. Not old, just mature. It's like his looks are as confident as his voice is. Strong, holding... mature.

"I just needed out," she responds.

"I could say the same about myself."

"There's nothing in there for me, anyway."

"Again, I could say the same." He sucks in a breath and then points to her wrap. "That's very...unique. Just absolutely beautiful. Handmade, right?"

Andrea slowly nods her head. It feels heavy, like if she were to nod any faster, her head would drop to the ground. But she continues to nod anyway. Not too many men would stop to appreciate brightly colored hand-crafted items, but here's a man, in the middle of the night, on a street where — is that a line of people marching behind the houses?

The marching and stomping get closer. She can hear the rhythm of their feet. It's difficult to make out their figures; they're all a blurry shade of blue.

"Well done," the man says, and his voice breaks her away from the marching line of blue people.

"Well done?" Confusion swims inside of her. It's racing in circles just like the stars above her.

"Yes, well done. Not everyone can pull off something so uniquely artistic. But you? You wear it well. I can tell that you have talent."

The line of blue people is closer now. Andrea can't understand how they ended up so close so quickly. She blinks again and they're marching next to her, sharing the same sidewalk she's standing on. They're so close that one of the bodies brushes a shoulder on hers. Yet, they don't acknowledge it. They keep marching to an awkward beat.

It's not until Andrea looks up at the face of one of these people does she realize there is no face looking back. Each head is covered by a blue hood, concealing their identities. It's one long mass of blue caterpillar people marching to the beat of their own choosing.

Andrea blinks and as quickly as the blue-hooded people arrived, they are gone. Behind her. Marching into the distance of her spot at Deuces and turning the corner out of sight.

"You are talented, aren't you?"

For the second time, the mystery man breaks her gaze from the blue people. This time, her eyes land back on him. She takes in his words. His compliments. His adoration for the thing she created. She never once heard her boyfriend mention it. He never admired her creativity. At most, he barked at her to clean up after herself because her *junk* was *taking up space.*

Andrea swallows. Maybe it's the alcohol swimming in her bloodstream. Or maybe it's the warmth of his eyes, but her insides feel like they are heating and curling up at the same time. Her insides are dancing like the stars above her.

"Do you do that a lot?" She tries to focus.

"Do I do what a lot?" His voice sounds like mud on oil.

"Agree to things so easily? Do you always compliment girls on the things that are important to them, or do you really get it? Get...me?" The jungle juice has taken over her head now and is shaking her thoughts into mushy jumble juice.

She takes another step forward and she can smell him now. He smells different...better than the myriad of booze and sweat inside the house.

53

The house that is only a few feet away, yet seems to be miles behind her now.

"Do you?" The words swim out of her mouth and spill into the open before she can catch them. "Do you get me?" They sound so desperate to her. Desperate for understanding, and attention her boyfriend never fully gives.

Before she can tell her body to stop moving, her free hand is on his chest. He is just as warm as his smile, and she wants to crawl into him, feel his skin wrap around hers, and melt into him until she is nothing more than a puddle that could evaporate in the sun.

"Tell me you get me."

An arm wraps around her and she melts. This is all she wanted, someone to hold her preciously and listen to her clumsy words fall out into the open. She can feel every muscle in her body melt into his. She almost drops the cup she had been holding onto, but this shadow-man must, in fact, be a mind reader because he takes it from her. Then, he takes his own full cup and pours it into hers.

"You were empty," he offers her.

Andrea nods. "But don't you want your own drink?"

"It looks like you could use it more."

That warm smile, those eyes. She was meant to get out of that house and find him here. He *does* get her.

She gives a smile back. A loose gift for his generous one. Then, for the fifth time tonight, she tips up her cup and downs whatever is inside.

Of course, it's jungle juice.

Andrea's body falls forward, knowing his arms would be there, welcoming her, holding her, giving her whatever it is she had been looking for to fill in the holes she had before tonight.

"Let's go somewhere special, k?"

She nods. That sounds good. The escape she had been hoping for.

"But first, let me take a long look at you." He stands her up straight.

54

Through blurry vision, she sees his gaze scan over her. His eyes land on her hair, where his eyebrows knit and irises widen.

Life spins now, in rocking ship waves and unknowing footing. So she closes her eyes to keep down the chips and salsa from earlier.

His hands roam. Not on her waist or around her sides like the boys inside the house, but behind her head and through her hair, raking the chestnut locks through his fingers.

She tips her head back and opens her eyes, watching the stars make circles and waves in the sky. It is like a beautiful painting actively drinking her in, engulfing her as his hands do the same.

Then, *snip*.

Her eyes refocus, now on him, her vision still blurry and understanding less candid. His fingers pinch in front of her, holding something wispy.

Hair. He had cut her hair.

Confusion sweeps over her as her eyes roll back and the starry night sky fades to black.

CHAPTER SEVEN

I step back from the chattering crowd, admiring my own handiwork.

"Is that what I think it is?"

"Is that *who* I think it is?"

"That's disgusting!"

"It's unbelievable!"

"The dean isn't going to like that very much…"

I smile at the mumbled voices around me. I had spent all last night in Livvy's dorm, listening to her reciting DNA sequences over Janelle's sobs while my hands went nuts on canvas. The only thing on my mind had been the conversation I overheard at Joe's and the sadness underlying Malory's voice. That memory and my imagination that filled in the gaps guided every color choice and every stroke of my brush.

If Creepy Crane had actually done what I think he did, then campus needs to know.

Students need to know.

Professors need. To. Know.

So yeah, the mega-sized canvas my paintbrush danced all over last night? Yeah, it's shocking. That's the whole point. None of this high school talk behind-the-back rumor nonsense. I'm going straight to the source, in the way I know how.

Thank you, Noland, for giving me a brush that can handle it.

So, there it is, right outside the physical education building, displayed under the last office window on the second floor. Doctor Crane's office, where everyone will see the truth of the man who watched them run laps, crunch their abdomens, and sweat through gym clothes a few times a week. Everyone takes Crane's physical education class. And when I say everyone, I mean *everyone*. No one stepped foot on Volga University who didn't end up in the greasy-haired, stanky breath, pit-stained professor's room with his eyes on them.

That's because we all had to. It was a requirement to take his physical fitness class during freshman year. And if somehow you glossed over that requirement, it came back to bite you on the rear the following year. No Crane class, no diploma. That's the Volga way.

And Crane always wore a big smirk because of that. Having every student enter campus grounds in his classroom meant having every *body* in his classroom at his disposal.

Makes. Me. Sick.

The circle of spectators grows thicker around the base of my artwork. It isn't the best I have ever made, but this is definitely the most attention anything I created ever got. Good. I am proud of that at least.

Behind the bobbing heads of students and their gasping mouths is a lifesize-ish painting that would and should make even Mel Ramos blush. And he nearly paved the way of naked ladies and appropriation in the form of art. Wonder Woman wasn't created to be a pin-up girl, but he made it work through simple brushstrokes dipped in pops of color, and people loved the heck out of it.

But this isn't some pop artist's cheeky rendering.

These painted bodies are proud and their bits and dangles are front and center. The man's fingers point to his erection in a demanding gesture and the woman's body curves to nearly straddling it between her own wiry legs.

And even though her body is womanly shaped with all the womanly curves, her face is far less mature than the rest of the painting would suggest. Yup, she has a baby face. And not as in the "oh she's so beautifully young and vibrant" type of baby face, but an actual face of a baby.

The eyes are closed shut and the mouth open wide, screaming out and crying in its baby agony. She is *The Scream*, hands over her face, pulling down the skin of her cheeks, unable to leave the position he posed her in. She is *The Scream*, caught in the desire to leave, end her movements, run away, stop.

Everything in the contoured face says the baby doesn't want this. The baby doesn't want to be undressed, touched, and prodded at. I mean, who would by an angry old man with a pointed nose and a voice that shakes the ground you walk on?

The body says one thing. The face says another. Note to men: if her face says no, it means no. Same as if she said it with her actual words.

End of story.

And the man's face? Well, that is none other than Doctor Rupert Crane himself. The man that forced everyone to enroll in his class, practice their jumping jacks, and be timed on a mile. The man who treated us all as impressionable high school gym kids at a time when we were all trying to learn how to be the respectable adults we were supposed to grow into.

The adults we are supposed to grow into. Not the adults we are. Because we aren't, not really. Especially not the freshmen. We are all still kids. And he took gross advantage of that.

Show me what you can do. Isn't that what he had said? What? Was he pulling girls — *girls* — like Malory aside to *teach them a thing or two*?

They are just kids. Babies, even. At least that's how I see them. That's how I see us. It's how I feel most of the time, like an infant trying to navigate this world and not really knowing how I fit in. Which is exactly why everyone is staring at the baby in front of them.

And Crane's face? It's twisted into a grin of sorts. The kind that tells you that he has won the prize he had his eyes on. No, not won, but taken. Taken the person he had wanted for himself and called a prize.

If college has taught me anything about real life is that no one takes rumors seriously. Everyone brushes them off with "boys will be boys" and "she's overreacting" and "things like that don't actually happen." Bull sheet. I know better. Rumors are always based on some version of the truth, and I'll do my damndest to make sure they know that. And now everyone on campus has to face those rumors head-on and see how much they are worth in their weight.

"Everyone! Move out of the way!" And there he is, the *legend* himself. He is using the same voice I remember him using to yell at us to run faster, move stronger, and yadda yadda yadda.

Good grief, I hated that class.

"I said move it!" Crane's whistle blows and I stepped back a few steps, doing my part to make way for *the king* himself. He should have a front-row seat to the spectacle, after all.

I watch his beefy form part the sea of students and reach the painted spectacle head-on. This is when I congratulate myself. Side by side, I got it right. Crane's painted expression is chef's kiss perfect compared to the real life thing, right down to the crooked nose. It's like he's looking in a mirror, and I couldn't be prouder of myself.

"I need to know who's responsible for this!"

The crowd's murmurs wash over the lawn. I'm curious to see who will speak up, if anyone even knows. No one shows any sign that they do.

"I *said* who is responsible for this trash?"

My face wrinkles in disgust. Of course he would call this trash. That's what all the dumb people thought when they saw a bunch of paint strokes on a painting. Or as Janelle called it, *boobs*. Meat-headed people didn't think past how a thing in front of them looked. This was trash and boobs. A juxtaposition I'm sure would make his head explode if he thought about it hard enough.

I kind of wish he would. Kaboom.

59

My expression must have made as much noise as my insides wanted to scream out, because, in a heartbeat, I hear, "Ellis! In my office!"

Busted. I yell back as loud as he yelled at me. "I'm pretty sure I know what goes on in your office, Crane. And I want nothing to do with that." I throw my hand to gesture to my masterpiece. No way would I be another baby for him to take.

"NOW!" he bellows, and I can see his skin tone turning ten shades of red, almost carmine. I make a note of that. Maybe next time I will use that color and match it up perfectly.

I cross my arms at his demand. There is no way I'm going to move from that spot. Not now, not ever. Watching Crane get his just desserts is exactly where I want to stand in this moment. Heck, I want this moment to last forever.

"Girl, you've done it this time, Emily Ellis." I nearly jump out of my skin when I hear Livvy's whisper snake into my ear. "Sorry," she apologizes at my jump. "I didn't mean to sneak up on you. I just heard the new Ellis masterpiece was making its mark and had to get a look. I gotta hand it to you, Mills. I've never seen anything like it. His face is even redder than I expected."

I shake off my surprise. "But you heard it at Joe's, too, right? And you know how things go. If it's happened once, it's happened a thousand times. You saw the look on Malory's face. It can't happen any more. Zero more times. That's the goal." I rub my chin. "But you're right. This really did take a few breaths away. I'm pretty proud of that."

"Ms. Ellis, a word please." That's when every ounce of pride in my heart drops. That isn't the smug Doctor Crane's voice bellowing at me. That's Noland. And the seriousness in his voice tells me that he's not so proud of the work I've displayed. The disapproval is devastating.

"Now."

"Yes, Professor."

This isn't an equal talking to me. This is an authority figure who is ready to put down the hammer on my nonsense, and I'm forced to accept it. I swallow the lump in my throat as I follow the only professor on campus whose opinion I hold higher than my own.

CHAPTER EIGHT

Noland's office always feels like home to me. The walls are covered in shelves that house rotating art pieces, all donated by students whose skills exploded under his mentorship. He's like a proud father, always making room for another piece to add to the display. Somehow, he ended up with an entire shelf dedicated to my newest doodles and prints. And somehow, that shelf never rotated. It just grew until it was overflowing. I'm convinced one day, it'll drip into another shelf altogether. That is, unless I royally screwed up my position as a favorite student with my latest stunt.

Nah, I didn't... did I?

And then there were static art pieces every art professor is probably obligated to have framed and hanging on the wall behind his desk. Salvador Dali's *The Persistence of Memory* with its clocks melting into droopy bits. Johannes Vermeer's *Girl With a Pearl Earring* who always seems to be staring me down every time I look at her. Van Gogh's iconic *Starry Night* is right next to Edvard Munch's *The Scream*. Everyone who's anyone has a special place in their heart for *The Scream*. What most people don't know is that it's a direct depiction of how an anxiety attack feels.

How I imagine Malory felt in Crane's grasp. And every other girl who might have been seeing him after hours doing who knows what.

I highly doubt Munch ever meant for it to become the pop culture icon it is today. If he had known his suicidal scream for help was just going to be carbon copied onto fridge magnets and canvas purses, I'm pretty sure he would have offed himself off a bridge before he would have even picked up his first paintbrush.

I hope my recent rendition at least kept to the original concept, honoring it a little more than kitschy roadside gifts.

"Ms. Ellis." Noland props his elbows on his desk.

A few papers bow underneath their weight. Art history exam papers that he should be spending his time grading instead of contemplating the kind of lecture he is about to give me, which is probably only going to fuel whatever canvas I'm going to tackle next. And whatever that is, I'm sure it'll end up in Noland's possession, right next to all of his other favorite paintings. When he lowers his voice and leans forward toward me, I can smell his aftershave. I like it because it's not musky like most men's. It's sweet and comforting. Like apple pie, with cheese on top.

"Ms. Ellis, I hope I don't have to explain why you're here in my office."

His voice sounds what I imagine a disappointed dad would sound like, not that I'd know. And I really want to apologize and wrap my arms around him and have him tell me that it's okay, that he understands what I've created and knows the importance of its message. But I don't ask for his forgiveness nor force a hug onto him, regardless of the fact that he's the one who taught me to make statements with my art. He's the one who has always encouraged me to use my talent in ways others don't. Or don't know how. I'm sure without even getting out of my seat, he understands that, right?

His facial features drop. My lips purse and I narrow my eyes. I am not stupid. Of course I know why I was called into his office. This was where he could pull me aside and tell me how disappointed he is, where he could pat me on the head and say, "I understand what you mean, but we can find a better outlet for your emotions." This was where he could help hone in on the resentment I held against Crane and help me find the right number to call or the right conversation to start or the right thing to do to get justice for the girls who have kept their (his) secret in fear. This was away from the chaos outside the physical education building. The chaos I created.

The chaos I wanted.

"You don't approve of my painting?"

For the first time in the three years I've known Noland, he frowns at me. Never before have I felt the disappointment reach deep inside of me and pull out a want—no; a need—for redemption. I don't want to just wrap my arms around him and apologize. I want to drop to my knees and beg for a new start. I want to ask him to straighten me out, point me in the right direction. I want him to rub my back and tell me it will be okay. Things will be okay. I will be okay.

Ew. I hate that feeling.

"You can't make a lifesize portrait of a professor doing inappropriate acts with a child." His voice sounds tired, like he had already had this conversation with me several times. But he hasn't. Ever. It was always, "You're doing a great job, Ellis," or, "See me in my office to talk more about your next project, Ellis." Never, "Don't make pornographic images of a professor you don't like, Ellis."

How am I supposed to know where to draw the line?

Rules don't apply when innocent girls — *girls* — aren't being heard as they're screaming that they've been taken advantage of. Okay, maybe Malory wasn't screaming, but she was saying it. I'm just screaming for her.

I should look at him with sad eyes and say, "Of course, I understand," and apologize. But instead, I say, "A baby, not a child," and correct his description of my masterpiece. If I'm going to go down for what it is, then it needs to be crystal clear as to what it actually is.

"And somehow that's better?" His tone is so scratchy and I wish I could smooth it out to its typical buttery sound.

I shrug. "I guess not better. But it definitely makes it louder. You saw what it did out there." I throw my finger to the door, and I swear if I

64

strain my ears enough, I can still hear the crowd chattering away, gasping for breath as they take in every inch of my statement. Every. Inch.

Noland nods, and I can see. He gets it. He knows. There's a piece of him that wants to pat me on the back, congratulate me, and somehow shrink my artwork to a size where he can proudly display it daddy-style on his shelf for everyone to see as they walk in. My fists want to pump themselves into the air because *he gets it*.

But then he doesn't get it. Without a word, he pulls his laptop open, slings his fingers across the keyboard a few times, and shuts the lid.

What the heck was that?

It was literally a couple of taps, and now things feel so final. He's done talking. Whatever he typed out in less than ten seconds has put my future in someone else's hands. Not the warm mentor I looked up to for three years. The same man who I had hoped would guide me into my first job with a glowing recommendation so I wouldn't have to go through the one hundred step interview process, pit stains and everything. I had been one of his most promising students. He said so himself on more than one occasion. A couple of taps and I literally morphed into a delinquent in his eyes. Crap.

I effed up.

And now I'm sitting in silence, waiting for a detrimental knock on the door I know is bound to come. He drums his fingers. I tap my toes. He shifts in his seat and tucks his long dark hair behind his ear. A piece breaks free and swings back in front of his eyes. I mimic the same motion with my hair, but there isn't a lot to push back. It's just a small wisp that fell out of one of my braids. My leg bounces. His eyes shift. Even with the drumming and the tapping and hair pushing and leg bouncing and eyes shifting... it's too silent. I have to break it.

"Did you see those brushstrokes, though? They were so smooth and precise, thanks to the brush you gave me." Of course, I have to break the silence by asking for praise.

What an idiot, Mills.

He sighs again and I can tell his voice is still laced with scratchy dissatisfaction. "It's not about the technique, Ms. Ellis."

"But it was good, right? Just like you showed us?"

"It's about knowing where the boundaries are on our campus."

I don't mean to, but I scoff. Hard. He chose to use the word *boundaries* which is exactly the point I was trying to make. I thought he had seen. I thought he got it. I thought he realized that and understood.

"Ms. Ellis. We have standards here at Volga University. We show respect to our fellow students and staff members. We show respect for our community environment. That kind of thing might be tolerated elsewhere. In fact, I know for sure there are plenty of people outside our school perimeters who would be happy to have this kind of thing hanging on their walls. But here? No one wants to walk past something that is so blatantly vulgar every time they walk to math class."

"Actually, it would be phys-"

"I know your potential, Ms. Ellis. You're extremely talented. Your hands know their way around a canvas better than almost anyone else, even..." He trails off as he swallows back whatever words were supposed to end that sentence.

I swear, he's looking at my fingertips when he says this, and I choke out a, "Thank-"

"But you need to learn there is a time and a place for things that shock. Your junior year of college with a well-respected professor as the center of your subject matter is not it."

"But, Noland-"

"It's. Not. It. Not the time nor the place." He gives me a look of pity. *Pity,* and I shrink half my size in this chair. "Dean Anderson is going to come in here. He's going to ask if you are the reason for the angry crowd outside the physical education building. He's going to tell you that you need to clean up the mess you made, and then he's going to give you a quick rundown of how things are about to go."

"And how are things going to go?" I ask him, using the same influx in the words he just spat out at me.

He takes a deep breath in and looks up at the ceiling. For a moment, I believe he's going to reach his hands out and hold mine. As if he were ready to guide me through what he's about to say with a gentle heart. He doesn't. Part of me is relieved.

But he does walk me through what to expect. "Look, Mills. At any moment Dean Anderson is going to come through that door. He's going to tell you that what you did, what you created, is unacceptable at Volga University. He's going to ask you to clean it up somehow. Get rid of it, take it away, and apologize like you mean it to Professor Crane."

"I'm not apologizing to Crane!" I cut him off, but he ignores it with a wave of his hand.

"He will ask you to apologize like you mean it."

He breaks in his thought. I huff, but I believe he's not done.

"Then he's going to mention court."

Freaking court? What the heck? Why would the dean bring me to court over a piece of art I placed on campus?

Noland must sense my anxiety spiking. Inside, I am *The Scream,* melting away into bendy oranges and blues and wanting so hard to pull myself together. But *court*?

He waves an arm in the air. "It's not like real court. It's campus court. And it's in front of a council of peers. They'll review your case, ask you to make a statement to defend yourself, and make a decision."

"The decision to keep my hard work displayed on campus?" I'm hopeful. Probably, too hopeful.

"The decision to keep *you* on campus."

I flump back into my chair. That hadn't even occurred to me. They'd kick me out? Like, for good? Goodbye, Volga University, and hello townie life? Where I'd be in danger of turning into a cranky old lady with coke-bottle glasses, yelling at college students for no real reason?

Well, crap. That's not what I meant to do.

I sit with this for a minute. What would it be like to no longer be a student? I'd stop going to classes. Find a new place to live. Try and make a living for myself doing the thing I like to do most? Work side by side with Stark at the craft store? That part wouldn't be so bad.

I think about the yellow paper Stark gave me. The art festival. Auction. Some of those pieces go for thousands. I don't know who in or around the small town of Volga has a thousand green bills just wasting away in their pockets. But if I could weasel myself into that gallery with my own set... I could maybe get a break.

All I need is four paintings. Four *good* paintings to submit.

And the people here would be able to hear my messages instead of shutting them out.

I make my decision right then and there, as a knock raps on the door. The dreaded knock I knew was going to happen, but makes me jump anyway.

Dean Anderson's gaze shoots darts through me. There is no way this is going to end with a simple request of moving my artwork and a measly apology.

I jolt to a stand and look Dean Anderson directly in the eye. Well, as directly as possible. That man is tall and I stand at a very average five foot five inches. But I look him directly in the eye anyway and blurt out, "I'm leaving. I'm not moving my art. I refuse to keep quiet, and I'm not going to plead my case in some makeshift court you've put together on campus. I'm leaving. I'll go. I'll find a place where my messages will be heard instead."

The Dean glares back down and all but pats me on the shoulder. "Ms. Ellis. I will deal with you later. Right now, I need to speak with Professor Elsinger."

Noland exchanges a look with Dean Anderson and the entire vibe shifts in the air. It's sticky, tense, and I sit back down in my seat to shrink into nonexistence.

It works. Sort of. For a moment, I'm just a kid in a seat while the men are talking above me and over me.

Dean Anderson breathes out a heavy sigh. Noland smolders a look back at him. It's a language of men I loosely understand, but could never speak myself. Something has happened. Something more important than my message. Isn't that always the case for women? And I sit there, silent, not asking in their language what's up. Not that I would know how to anyway.

Noland opens his mouth to speak, but before any words shoot out, the Dean does it for him.

"They found a body."

Noland's eyes morph from confusion to shock to despair and back to shock. There's a mixture of disgust in there, too, lightly. But it's mostly shock. "Excuse me?" he says.

"A girl. A student. Malory Gibbons. They found her body."

CHAPTER NINE

"I think I'm going to have to throw these clothes away when I get home." Stark pulls another rancid bag of trash out of the dumpster and more liquid filth drips out onto his pants.

It's gross. And sad. And the insides of my body are tearing into a billion pieces simply being here, especially with Stark inches away from me. This is not how I'd like to spend quality time with him.

This is where Malory was found. Her body tossed away by the dumpster, just like any of these trash bags. It's not fair. It's not okay. And somehow, I don't know how, I get the feeling it's all connected.

Malory's conversation at Joe's. My Crane painting. The beat-red face of Crane himself. Malory's death.

I can taste the sickness burning from my very core. Which is why I'm here. I want that painting back. It doesn't just belong to me. It belongs to the world.

"Thank you, Stark." I breathe out. "Thanks for coming with me. Here. At these dumpsters to dig elbow deep in this mess for me."

He gives me a wink. "Well, you made it clear it's not just for you. It's for that girl, too."

"And others."

"And others," he agrees. "So, in the name of justice and art, I'm happy to be here, even if it means I'll walk away smelling like fish sticks and," he points his nose out like a Golden Retriever and sniffs, "stale booze." He pulls out another bag and wrinkles his outstretched nose, tossing the trash on the ground. "When was the last time the dining hall served fish sticks anyway?"

"Last Thursday," I say. "Every Thursday is fish stick day. Toward the end of the week, the cooks get a little lazy and desperate when most of the good stuff is already used up."

"I see."

We work in silence for a few minutes. Bag after bag full to the brim of empty beer cans, vomit-soaked rags, and who knows what else collect on the ground around us. I feel sticky, sweaty, and I probably stink worse than my nose can actually pick up.

When I reach back in and remove another soaking wet bag full of mysterious substances, it's no use. The dumpster is empty of Crane's face, the baby's expression, or any boobs. I toss what I'm holding back in the dumpster and shake my hands off of the goop they had collected.

"Unfortunately, it looks like you might have gotten messy for no reason. It's not here." I brush my hands on my pants and realize I will probably have to toss my clothes away, too. "I thought for sure it would have to be here. Not that it really matters. I'm not sure what I would do with it if I found it. I mean, it's not like it's evidence or proof that Crane has actually done anything. No one on campus is going to see it as anything but a disturbing canvas they don't want to be displayed." My body slumps, resting against the walls that semi-enclose around the dumpsters.

I can feel Stark thinking, even though he says nothing. He holds up a finger to me as if to say, "Wait a minute," and walks back to the dumpster, rummaging his hands behind it.

My eyes scan around my feet. What did we get ourselves into? Dumpster diving in the middle of the day for something that probably isn't here? The police probably picked the scene clean the moment they came out to inspect, gather, and report. I'm sure they wanted to leave it as spick and span as possible. No parent wants to pay for their kid's college tuition with a dead body in sight.

I close my eyes and picture Malory. Her dark brown hair pulled back by a brightly colored headband. Red. Orange. Yellow. Sometimes even blue. I block out the sounds around me; students walking to the dining hall, chatting about projects and papers and exams, the thought of a girl who died only days ago fades in the distance. And I recall the conversation my ears tuned into so intently at Joe's.

Every noise around me fades away and all I can hear is Malory's voice. Scared. Small. Nervous to speak out loud. Her whisper-yell echoes within me. "It's not like that. I had to." What did she mean by this? Why did she have to?

I imagine her eyes, scared. Her mouth, twisted. Her body moving away from whatever she *had* to do.

I imagine her being *The Scream* itself, twisted and tormented inside. And yet, no one around her saw her for the truth inside. Not even the person she was openly confessing to.

And then Mariëtte's voice breaks into my memory, too. Her response is light, and airy. It's as if she's joking, poking fun at this girl in front of her. "Was he at least a gentleman?"

Bile builds up in the back of my throat and I clench my eyes shut even harder. Internally, I answer Mariëtte. "No gentleman would make anyone feel forced to do anything."

Screeeeeetch.

Stark has used his brute strength to shift the dumpster away from the wall behind it, breaking the recorded conversation replaying in my head. He is hunched over, scouring the uncovered ground behind the dumpster, and I'm standing like an idiot, staring at the ground. The ground. The dirty, smelly, sticky ground. Where crushed cans, banana peels, and forgotten headbands go to die.

Headbands. Could it be? There, right by my feet is a bright blue headband. The same kind — the same one? — Malory wore the last time I saw her. I scoop it up and feel the fabric. It's stained in one area, but it's still soft, well-loved by the would-be wearer. One circular piece of fabric that would have given purposeful comfort day in and day out.

I wrap it around my wrist. This makes it real. This makes it all the more important to find this painting and hold onto what I can of Malory.

"Wheet-woo," a whistle breaks my thoughts. "Hey, Mills! I'm not sure if this is what you're looking for, but…"

That's right. Stark's here. And he's still searching for my painting while my scattered brain has moved on to trying to make sense of why I really am here and if it's enough to actually do anything justice. If the police aren't releasing anything and there's only speculation of — of what? Food poisoning? Heavy drinking? It doesn't matter what speculation there is. There's a piece of Malory's story in here and I need to find it. It's the only piece that no one is talking about, especially Mariëtte Dunn, the Alpha Big Sister.

"Does this happen to look familiar?"

My eyes shoot up. Stark is squeezing his body out from the small opening he made behind the dumpster. Sweat collects on his shirt and a bead of it drips down his arm. A few side steps out and he produces a large canvas, complete with the baby face and what should be Crane's scowl.

"Oh, Stark, I could kiss you!"

I grab hold of his shoulders and squeeze. They're damp and strong. It's like holding onto a couple of sweet grapefruits under his sleeves. That's a weird analogy, but it's all I can think of in the moment where my hands are on him and he is standing still. His eyes twitch at the sides, and for the split second they lock onto mine, I'm afraid he's going to actually take me up on that offer and lean in, but he doesn't. He just smiles and pushes the corner of the canvas toward me.

Bummer, Crane's face doesn't look like his anymore. Some of the wet mush in the dumpster must have seeped out and dripped all over his corner of the painting. Now, it's a blur of peachy skin tones, blackish streaks, and sunburnt oranges. His face is wiped clean. His identity gone. Its message is half erased, but it's here, and it's in my hands. And even with the stains that blur it, I have no doubt it still speaks some truth in its art.

"So, this is the famous painting I've heard about?" Stark moves away from me and the painting and lifts a hand to his chin. "Yeah, I can see where this might get you in trouble." He gives a deep chuckle that tells me he's a little amused by my choice of subject.

I flinch. "Yeah, it did. Did Livvy tell you I need to find a place by next week?"

"She said you're gonna have to do campus court."

"Yeah, that ain't happening, Stark."

"Why? You don't want to defend yourself? Your art?" He sounds concerned.

I let out a long breath and shake my head. "Not if it means sucking up an apology and acting like it never happened. I think there are better ways of defending it than compliance."

Stark nods and runs a hand across his forehead. "Like the gallery?" He sucks his bottom lip in and nods again. "This would definitely get some attention at the gallery."

"Well, yeah; anything with boobs will get attention."

He stifles a laugh. "Well, sure, but that's not what I mean. I mean that Livvy's right. You have real talent here. I'm not just saying that because she's my sister and I have to say she's right. I'm saying that because I've met all the artists in this town and none of them are this good. Compared to what I'm seeing here, they don't hold a candle. This," he gestures to the painting, "this is supposed to be seen. Not just for the content," he chuckles again, "but for the craftsmanship, too."

"You think?"

"I know."

Somehow, we've ended up a few inches closer. I can see his jawline tighten when he swallows back a little. I try to tell my feet to move back, away, give him some room. Clearly, he doesn't need his kid sister's friend getting all up in his personal space. But they don't move. I'm stuck to the spot, holding onto my painting, locked onto Stark's jawline and trying to ignore the smell of week-old fish sticks. That last part is pretty impossible. It's worse than skunk spray, and I'm pretty sure it's going to stay in my clothes just as long, if not longer.

Then, I feel something on the side of my face. My hair. The little strands that have made their way out of my braids and have turned into little wisps of fuzz. I'm sure I look a sight. No doubt, my face has dirty gunk that dripped from one or two of these bags. And I'm sure my hair is sticking out at all ends like a ratty blonde halo.

But that's not my hair I feel tickling my face. It's actually Stark's hand. His fingers have found that little wisp and are now stroking it like some kind of prized possession. A moment goes by or an eternity, I can't tell which, and he finally tucks that strand behind my ear so I no longer feel anything loose from my braid.

"Sorry," he says. "It looked in your way. I wanted to fix it." I swear he blushes as he grabs hold of another part of the painting. "Here, let me help you with this."

We work together, easing the canvas away from the trash and dirt. Some of the debris falls off on its own and some we have to pry off, crossing our fingers that most of the paint stays intact. Luckily, it does. When we finally get it out and free of the dumpster junk, Stark helps me over to my skateboard. I step a foot onto it, ready to balance myself and my painting back to my dorm room where I'll contemplate wherever I'm supposed to go next.

Just as I place my foot onto the board, I hear a single voice. She's yelling. Commanding.

"Step to it, ladies! Single file!"

A fit looking blonde is leading a pack of girls in Alpha pink single file down the sidewalk.

"Ladies! I want to hear you answer me loud and clear. Got it?"

"Yes, Big Sister Mariëtte!"

Oh, so that's what this is. This is the big sister herself in action, guiding these girls into… what?

"Who is the one authority you must listen to at all times?"

"You, Big Sister Mariëtte!"

Oh, she's guiding them into her dictatorship. Got it.

"Good. And whose voice do you follow when a new rule is made?"

"You, Big Sister Mariëtte!"

She likes to repeat herself, doesn't she?

"That's right. And who do you promise to respect and obey with no questions asked?"

"You, Big Sister Mariëtte!"

Note: This is exactly what I mean when I say sororities are like cults. The same question three times in a row. Look to the leader, do whatever stupid thing they do, and don't ask any questions. Wear what they wear, say what they say, and keep any weird mojo stuff you do together a secret from the world.

"And if I tell you to be happy, you smile. If I say something funny, you laugh. If I tell you to cry, you show me the biggest crocodile tears possible. And if I tell you to kick butt? You kick it to the curb and back, never to be seen again. Am I clear?"

"Yes, Big Sister Mariëtte!"

"Good girls!"

She stops the line from moving further with the palm of her hand out in front of her. The single hand has each girl in Alpha pink stopping in sync. They all stare at her, waiting for her next command. Tension fills the air as it seeps out of the girls and into the open. In this silence, someone comes running toward them from the other side of the sidewalk. She's not in Alpha pink, but she's making her way straight toward Mariëtte. She's moving with purpose, each foot pounding the pavement to close the distance between them.

As she gets closer, I recognize this girl in denim. She's no Alpha or Beta or Zeta or any other -a. She's Sam. The sassy girl from art class.

I didn't know she was friends with the alpha Alpha.

I can't hear them talk. Sam's too quiet for that. She's not going to yell out to anyone out in the open like the pink girls just were. Speaking of, all those pink girls are still standing still as statues in their line. They're waiting for a release signal their Sister hasn't yet given.

A few minutes of this chat and I can tell Mariëtte is starting to get loud again. I can't tell if she's ready to release her little statues or start up a war with Sassy Sam. Her face crinkles up and she takes a deep inhale.

"Alright girls!" Her hand goes up again. She's about to release them.

But Sam interjects. She moves her mouth, and Mariëtte turns her head to listen.

"You're next, Aleah!"

With that, her hand closes and all the pink girls start up their engines. Each foot moves in step, and as they march away from my line of sight, I can hear one more, "Yes, Big Sister Mariëtte!" chorus.

I can feel how far my chin drops. It nearly scrapes the ground. I had thought Mariëtte was a little off at the coffee shop. But this? Ordering around a line of girls to laugh, cry, and smile without any questions asked? That's just... well, that's just bizarre.

"Well, that was interesting." Stark's voice is dry and I bet he feels just as weird as I do about what we just witnessed.

"Interesting is right. You know some people think she had something to do with Malory."

Maybe I'm phishing. Well, no. There's no maybe about it. I am phishing. I need to know what Stark thinks about that.

77

I look at my painting. I know for sure Crane's hands have something to do with Malory, both before and after her death. He has to be a part of it. But Mariëtte's response to Malory's confession? Her orders for girls to smile and be happy on command? I don't know. Something is up with her and I don't trust it.

I guess I don't trust a lot.

I'm aware I have issues.

"You mean Andrea, right?"

My stomach does flip floppy loops. No, I did not mean Andrea. I don't know who the heck Andrea is, and I'm afraid to ask, "Who?"

"The girl they found the other day?"

"No. The girl they found last week."

My eyes go wide. His eyes go wider. And now we're two owls staring at each other with the realization that there are now two dead girls in the small town of Volga. I curse myself for being so involved in my own junk that I didn't even realize it. I should have been paying closer attention to what's going on around me.

"Why didn't I know about this? Why didn't I hear about Andrea?"

Stark hangs his head. It's like he's ashamed to be the one to break this news to me. He shoves his hands into his pockets. I imagine his fingers rubbing against each other the same way they rubbed my hair. It gives me goosebumps. "From what I hear, her family didn't want it to be all over the news. They wanted to be able to mourn quietly, by themselves, without people asking them a million questions."

I shake my head. "But what about all the busy-bodies going in and out of those frat houses? Wouldn't someone have noticed?"

He shrugs. "I guess whoever walked by her thought she was drunk and passed out. She was a townie, after all. It's not like most students pay attention to those who aren't their own."

That makes sense.

Start continues, "On frat row, behind one of the houses. They think it was food poisoning or something like that. Maybe too much to drink. Again, I don't know much about it, because the family-"

"Wants to keep it quiet," I finish, quietly.

I cannot believe how this news got away from me. I feel so stupid for not being aware. Suddenly, the weight of the canvas feels like it's doubled, and I can barely hold it up. Malory's story is now fading into Andrea's. Something is happening. My feet falter into staggered steps.

"It's okay. Let me help you." He takes it from me and motions for me to lead the way, back onto campus.

Back to my dorm. Back to what feels like purgatory, waiting to figure out what's happening on campus and off, and somewhere in between, how the stories of two dead girls have gone completely missing.

CHAPTER TEN

Deuces feels so strange during the daytime. Each of the houses on frat row stands two stories high with large windows and balconies that look over the street. Usually, at night, they're filled with the silhouettes of drunken college kids wildly flailing their arms in the air while the base of whatever music is playing leaks through the walls and out into the open. I imagine the insides of the houses are coated with unnamed stains and smells that not even bleach can get rid of.

And every time I've passed by this row of houses, I've seen strange things. Weird things. Things like color-coordinated people dancing in circles or running laps on the lawns. Sometimes, they even covered their faces in strange masks or hoods.

I'll never understand Greek life.

But now, in the daylight, these houses almost look like they belong in some suburban housewife's dream. It's like these houses are wearing a mask during the day, just waiting for the darkness to roll in and let loose.

This isn't my normal jam. I've never actually been to any of these parties. No one has ever bothered to give the sarcastic art girl an invite.

Do you even need an invite to these things?

My phone buzzes in my back pocket, and without even looking, I know who it is.

"Hey, Livvy."

"Girl, how are you doing? Stark said you spaced after your dumpster diving episode, and you've been quiet for a few days. I'm worried. You okay?"

"Yeah, I'm alright. It's just that, I don't know. Isn't it weird?"

"The Andrea girl?"

"And Malory."

"And Malory," she echoes. I can feel the weight of her voice add to the weight I feel.

"I mean two girls in just over a week are murdered right here in Volga? That doesn't make sense. It's scary. And sad."

I step off the sidewalk and into the side yard of one of the houses. This is where she was. This is where they found her. According to Stark, several people passed her up after leaving Deuces on the walk of shame. It wasn't until the first Friday morning class that anyone bothered to stop and see if she was okay. And the person who found her? None other than Kyle himself.

I sit crisscrossed on the grass and ease my backpack off my shoulder. Inside are my supplies, paints, a canvas, and the brush Noland gave me.

I had been sitting in my dorm room for a few days in silence. Biding the time until my stupid campus court date. I could go to that, plead my case and all, but there really isn't much of a point. I've already made my decision. I'm leaving campus the second I find a place to go.

But first? This.

"You know, they haven't exactly said that it's murder, Mills. You might be jumping to conclusions." Livvy is always the voice of reason.

"No, they haven't, but it would be a pretty wild coincidence if something like food poisoning was dropping everyone like flies. Something tells me that's not it, Livvy."

"Well, you've eaten the dining hall food, haven't you?" I know Livvy is trying to lighten the mood, but even the worst mush on the dining hall trays doesn't do that kind of damage.

"Liv..." I sigh.

"Remember the time you got sick off the nacho bar?"

"Yeah. I lived in the bathroom for three days straight."

"You told me you felt like you were dying in there."

"Well, you would say the same if you felt like you had a meat grinder in your stomach."

She gives a light laugh. "So... maybe it's just a horrible coincidence?"

I breathe in a gulp of air. The scent of freshly cut grass tickles my nose. I wonder who cut the grass and how soon it was after Andrea was found. Did they push the mower with a heavy heart? Did they la-de-da over the area with headphones in? Did they care at all?

"I don't know, Liv. This just...it doesn't *feel* right, you know?

I can hear her sigh. "I know. It's scary. I just don't want to believe there's someone here in Volga who wants to hurt anyone else."

"I know what you mean."

I unzip my backpack and take out its contents. Everything lines up in front of me. My own little mobile studio. I close my eyes and picture what it must have been like, laying on the grass, probably at night. Was she alone? Did anyone try to help her?

The name Andrea Shepherd isn't familiar because she wasn't a student on campus. So who could she have been? Did she live nearby? Did she attend one of these parties? Or was she just passing through, just to happenstance the end of her life on this spot?

The story goes, according to Stark, that she was young. Passing for a college student even though she wasn't. So it's entirely possible she could have walked by at any point in time to blend in with any group who was there, much like Stark himself if he ever wanted to.

The only reasons why people actually go to frat parties is to blow off steam or drink away their stress. If she wasn't a student, she probably had some serious stress to end up here, on the lawn, alone and face up to the sky. Or maybe she was feeding into her curiosity while trying to escape from...well, I guess from whatever.

I adjust my position, stretch my legs out, careful to avoid all my materials, and lay back. The grass tickles my neck where my pulled back hair leaves it exposed. My eyes open and all I can see is the blue sky. A few white clouds speckle the image in front of me, and a couple of birds fly across it to land on a nearby tree.

I wonder if Andrea saw that tree. I wonder if she watched the birds, too. I wonder if she laid here under the stars and watched them watch her.

"Mills, you still there?"

Even with the phone still pressed to my ear, I forgot Livvy was on the other line, waiting for me to say something. Clearly, I'm a little lost in this space and need to find a way to find myself. Or rather, find Andrea. I guess that's why I brought all the supplies with me.

"I'm here, Liv. I just. I think I need to go paint."

"I get it, Mills. Just don't, I don't know, don't get too wrapped up in this, you know? You've got other things to worry about like where the heck you're going to live if you're actually leaving school. I don't want you to end up in something too deep and end up living on the streets."

I chuckle back at her. I already feel deep in this thing. Whatever this thing is. "I'm good, Livvy. Promise."

"Good luck painting."

I hang up and breathe in deeply again. I have no doubt whatever happened to Andrea happened at night, when either no one was looking or anyone nearby was too busy with beer, music, and whatever else was happening inside these houses. And it just sucks that no one can really say.

But being here, breathing the same air, feeling the same grass, possibly watching the same birds, maybe I can help with part of her story. Just a piece that no one else is considering. She may not be able to use her own voice, but I can paint a glimpse as to what it might have been like.

So, I think about what it might have been like. If she was leaving one of these houses with a cup full of who-knows-what that she emptied into her system, her head was probably swimming. Maybe she was dizzy. Maybe she'd throw her head back to the sky and let it wash over her. Maybe her eyes danced in her skull, making the stars move into swirly shapes she couldn't understand. And maybe someone was there with her, ready to take advantage of her unsure state of mind.

The tip of my brush dips into the first color. Deep blue. I mix it with black and I slather the entire canvas in the deepening color. Dark. It was dark. So dark, she probably couldn't make out the facial features of a person in front of her. Not unless she was up front, up close, and already within danger's grasp. As the brush strokes cover every corner, I can feel the darkness wash within me. I am here, but not here as in here, during the safety of daylight.

I'm here as in how Andrea was here, staring at the night sky forming in front of me. Grey streaks mark the shadows of clouds, wispy and long. And dingy yellows mark where the stars would have moved in front of Andrea's drunken eyes.

I'm convinced there's magic in this brush because I can *feel* Andrea. Without ever having known her, I can feel her voice ring through me. This was her last view, and it hurt.

My brush stabs at the canvas, taking away my own ability to decide where it goes. And before I know it, it's back in the black paint and scratching a large image in the corner. Tall, looming. It's like the tree I could see while laying back. Stick like limbs jut out, reaching forward, reaching for Andrea. Wanting to hold her.

Not hold, grab.

One limb develops a claw-like hand, and all of a sudden, it's not a tree, but a tree-like man. A shadow of a man, looming over her and grabbing for what he wants. Her. Her life.

A few more strikes of the brush and the painting is complete.

I breathe out a sigh, and take it in.

Heat burns in my stomach and my throat closes. It's Van Gogh reminiscent with a dark truth behind it.

I toss the canvas on the grass, and hug my knees to my chest. I don't even know why I feel like I need to know about her. I don't know why I need to record the piece of Andrea's story that makes sense to me. But I do.

So why does this hurt so much? I didn't even know this girl, I had never met her, and it hurts.

I hug myself tighter, and allow my stinging eyes to leak.

Ugh, this sucks. It sucks so much. I sit like this a while, letting the life of the painting wash over me and into me. I feel the pieces of her story that make sense to me. And as each piece of her story makes a stitch into my heart, I hold onto myself so that I can hold onto it.

"Whoa, um, did you do that?"

I pull my emotions together, swallow them down, and look up. Cuz I'd rather not have to explain why I'm crying over a girl I hadn't met.

It's Kyle. In his standard Zeta blue. Great.

I nod my head.

"That's really…creepy," he tells me.

"Not as creepy as it could be." Because as much as the painting in front of me holds a creep factor, it definitely doesn't hold a candle to the reality behind it.

He scratches his head as if I just gave him the riddle of a lifetime. "What do you mean?"

But I'm too emotionally exhausted to explain it to him. He's probably still wearing off the alcohol from the previous night and wouldn't understand anyway. And since he was the one to find Andrea here, I'm sure that he's got his own stuff he needs to work out. I'm on my own with this one.

"Hey, aren't you the girl that did the painting on campus? The one with the um…" He doesn't want to finish that sentence, so I do it for him.

"Boobs. With the boobs."

He blushes. "Well, yeah, that, but also with that creepy professor."

It's hard to read his expression, but it could be that he is impressed. Not just with the naked lady, but with the message behind the Crane painting. Maybe he would understand it if I took the time to explain what was going on.

"I mean, I've heard the rumors, too. I don't want to believe them, but I've heard he takes girls into his office one-on-one and they come out, you know."

"No; I don't know," I say honestly. "I can only imagine."

"Well, sweaty. And they're as young as freshman, girls who don't know they can say no to a professor. I think what you did is pretty awesome."

"Yeah?" Am I hearing this right? This meathead of a guy is actually showing recognition of my work? Not just gasping and gaping, but actually hearing the reason for its existence?

"Look, I don't know if you could use it or not…" Kyle reaches into his pocket. I'm impressed with how deep it is. Men's jean pockets always have more space than their female counterpart. He pulls out something oddly familiar. A knobbly handle fits inside his fist, and on the end of it is a little tuff of bristles.

"Where did you…?"

"Get this?" he finishes for me. "Weird thing is, I kinda like found it. It was just laying out in the art building hallway. When I asked Prof-Noland about it, he just shrugged. I would have thought it was his based on his weird brush cleaning lesson, but-" Kyle shrugs himself. "But, I guess it was up for grabs. I tried using it for my last project, but I've gotta be honest. I don't know what I'm doing."

86

Then Kyle uses the handle to point to my painting. "You clearly do, though. You've got talent. So if you think you could use this, then it's all yours." He offers the handle to me.

With a steady hand, I accept his offer. If the other brush could create the starry painting in front of me with ease, I can only imagine what two of these artisanal brushes could help me create.

My fingers play with the bristles. They're just as soft as the first brush. No. They're actually softer. They're an auburn brown, with little bits of red mixed in. Definitely a completely different brush, but a sister of the first.

"Thanks, Kyle. I appreciate it." And I do. I really, really do.

"Well, yeah." But he doesn't hold his gaze on me for too long because good 'ol Janelle is running down the sidewalk, calling him.

"Kyle! Kyyyy-le!"

That's when I decide it's probably time I get off the ground and pick up. I have no idea if these two are at the on-again part of their relationship yet, but even if they are, it's almost worse than the off-again moments.

I begin to pack up my paints, placing them one by one back into my backpack. Somehow, I feel lighter for having used them to create something new and heavier for what I created. I'm just hoping this holds as much meaning to others as it does to me.

And if Kyle can see that in my Crane painting, I bet others can see it in my Andrea canvas.

"Kyle! Hey baby!"

It's on-again.

She wraps her arms around his neck and forces her body against his. I guess the entire world outside of the two of them went blank because she doesn't acknowledge I'm only six feet away while she presses her mouth against his and begins to suck face like the world is ending.

I put the last jar of paint back in my bag and pocket my paint brushes. The only thing left is the wet canvas, which will have to dry on my board-ride back.

The lovebirds in front of me separate their mouths with a pop. It's gross. I'm ready to get out of here. But then the world around them must have come back into view because Janelle sees me.

"Hey. You're Olivia's friend."

"Livvy."

"Yeah. You're her friend, Emily, right?"

"Mills."

"Haven't you been kicked off campus?"

Kyle's mouth drops open. "I didn't hear that. Are you really? Kicked out of school?"

"Well, not exactly," I don't feel like getting into the semantics of it. "But, yeah, I'll be out of Volga University in a little bit."

"Oh, that sucks."

Janelle slugs him in the arm.

"Ow," he whines and rubs it. Then, he turns to me, "Do you have a place to go? I mean, you're not going to live on the streets or anything, are you?"

Janelle slugs him again.

"What's that for?" he whines a second time.

"What? Are you offering for her to crash at the house or something? Let her stay close by? Just like you did with...with that *girl*?"

I may have just witnessed these two switch into the off-again phase right in front of me.

"I told you nothing happened!"

"Bull. I know you were sleeping with her! I told you, if I catch you around her again..."

Kyle's face goes red. I should pick up my canvas and slink away right now.

"Don't talk about Malory like that!" Kyle looks more hurt than angry. And did he just drop Malory's name so casually?

"Oh, I bet you don't want me to talk about her." Janelle crosses her arms and swings her back toward Kyle in a huff. "Still defending her? Even now?"

"It's not like that, Jan. It's just that... that..."

"I told you, if I saw you around her again, I'd-"

"Cut her head off and throw it in the river..." I don't mean for it to slip out, but it does. I want to swallow those words back the second I hear them out in the open.

She glares at me, silent.

I wish I could vanish from here. Just poof myself and my canvas away from the deathly beams she's shooting at me.

"That's not what you meant, though." Kyle rubs Janelle's arm. "That's not what she meant," he assures me.

And now I have no idea what to think. I know Janelle seems a little unhinged at times, but could she have really hurt another girl? Over Kyle? Was that enough reason? Malory wasn't exactly found in the lake, but a threat like that makes me wonder.

"Look," Kyle addresses me again while holding onto Janelle's shoulders, "if you're in a bind-"

Janelle huffs.

Kyle's voice thins out in an annoyed strain, "Then you might want to check the old house down the way." He shoots a thumb to point down the street. "It's no two story paradise, but it's up for rent. It goes back up on the renter's market every few months or so and usually sits there for a while until someone decides to shell out the money for it."

At the realization that Kyle is, in fact, not inviting me to sleep in his bed next to him, Janelle turns around to face him with a beaming smile on her face.

"Just saying, you might want to check it out," Kyle finishes his thought.

"Thanks," I ease out as I bend out to pick up my canvas. A bit of sticky paint rubs off onto my thumb, but it doesn't change a thing. I still feel the heaviness in it. I still feel Andrea's voice. "Yeah, thanks," I repeat.

Because maybe this really is the opportunity to let these messages out into the open. Maybe a crappy house down the street is exactly the space I need to paint them for the world to see. And maybe the art show is exactly where they need to be seen.

CHAPTER ELEVEN

"You sure this is a good idea, Emily Ellis?" Livvy's concerned tone fills my ears, and I see why.

The house in front of us, my soon-to-be house, the house that will keep me in Volga so I can keep doing my art 'thang' is...well, let's just say the term *house* is being generous. The windows are dark and smudged, and did I mention dark? And it isn't from something as fancy as blackout curtains. The actual glass has somehow aged to the point where I can't see through them at all.

At least that will save me money. I don't have to buy curtains. Or blinds. Or any other fancy pants window dressing.

The siding is barely hanging on. The door looks like it's going to fall off its hinges, and when I step on the front porch, it feels spongy.

The whole thing looks like it's melting. It's my melting house.

I nod vigorously. "Yup. It's all mine!"

I can hear her exhale in disbelief, and part of me can't believe it either. The whole thing might crumble on top of me, but this is what I can afford. It's all mine.

"You told me it was a great idea, even if it did come from Kyle," I remind her. "Besides, the representative from the rental company is already inside. All I need to do is hand over my signature."

She wrinkles her nose. "I dunno, Mills. I don't think a signature is going to make this place liveable."

"Okay." I roll my eyes. "Maybe it needs some paint. Some love. Some extra TLC here and there."

She looks like she's going to jump out of her skin climbing up to the front porch with me. The box of things in her hand is audibly shaking, and I'm excited to see what Stark found in his tiny apartment to give pitiful 'ol me, but I will wait to dig into those treasures.

"Come on," I encourage her. "Maybe it'll be more impressive inside."

And it is, a little. The hardwood floors are clean, the kitchen includes working appliances, and there's even a table and chairs included. The front entrance also has a large clock big enough to tell the time from nearly anywhere in the open floor plan. It's also funky enough for my taste. Its shape is warped. More like a wobbly moon than a circle, and it bows forward just enough to make it feel like the slightest touch will drop it from the wall.

It's not just my melting house. It's my melting clock house.

Livvy places her box of things on the table so gently, I think she's testing to see if it will collapse under the weight. It doesn't, and I have to admit, I'm a little relieved that it's standing just fine.

I mean, the exterior didn't exactly set a high bar of expectation, but this is roughly liveable. There's no mold in the bathroom and the walls aren't caving in yet. If only I can find a place to do art, a place where I could find the spark of inspiration I need and hone in on it. But I suppose that will come later.

"I know, it's not exactly a palace, but we've been patching up the holes and have a plumber on hand for the pipes. And like you said over the phone, you can't beat the price anywhere else over here."

Mr. Ritten has a nice face, the kind that says he does his best to be an honest man where he can, so I believe him when he says he's been patching up the pieces of the house that need it most.

I also believe him that there isn't another rental property in town with this low of a price tag. I mean, I can't imagine there would be another place quite like it in a twenty-mile radius.

"Where's the dotted line?" My trigger finger feels itchy and if I think about it much longer, I might lose my nerve, lose out of the deal, and end up back home at Samhale trying to convince Mom that I'm not a deadbeat loser whose mouth got her in trouble, again.

The stack of papers is bigger than I expected. And, honestly, I'm not reading all the fine print above and below the lines where it says Signature.

Does anyone pay attention to that stuff anyway?

When I get to the three thousandth page, I hand over the brick of papers with a smile. "All done!" I say.

He holds out a hand for me to shake. "Thank you so much, Ms. Ellis. Mr. Elsinger will be pleased."

My brain twitches, hearing an oddly familiar name, but it doesn't take hold in my thoughts. There could be a million Elsingers in Volga county. A family name that was born here ages ago and will die here when the Earth decides to implode on itself. There are plenty of people in Volga whose entire lineage fits within the county perimeters.

It doesn't matter anyway. This house is now mine.

Well, as "mine" as it can get for being a renter.

And that's when I do something I don't remember ever doing before. I grab Livvy's elbows and shake her arms silly. I pinch my eyes shut and shake my head, and an unbelievably loud squeal erupts from inside of me.

Livvy and I are jumping up and down, her squeals mimicking mine. And together, we're nearly dancing in the tiny kitchen, proving that the floors actually can take the beating of two people putting their whole weight on them.

In this moment, we could probably pull off Alpha pink just fine.

"What do we do first?"

Livvy sniffs at my clothes, still holding onto a hint of dumpster diving memories between their fibers. Then she points to the far end of the room. "My guess is that you haven't bothered washing the few clothes you own, Mills. Maybe this is the perfect chance to try out that washing machine over there."

I laugh. She laughs. I have my own washing machine. There's not a single person on campus who could say that, so I'm already a step above where I was before.

CHAPTER TWELVE

Him

I'm not okay. Not anymore. Not after doing this three times with no success. I still haven't cracked the code on how to be better. Do better. Be better. I'm definitely doing fine. But fine isn't enough. Fine isn't going to get me into the realm of possibilities. Fine isn't going to give me the recognition my body craves.

This *thing* at my feet. This squirming, crying *thing* has got to be it. It's got to do the trick. It's got to be my ticket out of here. Because if this *thing* doesn't do it, then there's only one more option. And that option? Well, I don't want to have to use *her* for it. She's meant for more. She's meant to be a master as well, not a recruit.

A recruit should be just enough to work and yet someone — *something* — I can let go of easily. Like the thing on the floor.

It whimpers.

"Did you drink up?" I ask.

I watched it drink. Gulped the glass down even. But that was yesterday and I need this *thing* gone. Out of here. I have plans for this space and I know for sure I can carry out those plans. Someone new is taking over. The dotted lines are signed. I can't have any of my trash rotting away down here for her to find. There's just no time for dilly-dallying or nonsense waiting games. I got what I needed and now I need it out of here.

And gone completely. Because if I have the one thing…

I slip two fingers into my back pocket and feel the tuff between them. Both soft and prickly, it's perfect. I can only imagine what this lock can do. What it'll unlock. It's so worth it. All of it. This is what will get me accepted.

If that doesn't work…

No. That won't happen. It can't happen. I won't let it happen.

It groans again.

I groan back. "Need another drink?"

I walk over to the little cabinet next to my gas stove, fling the door open, and hear it crack against the wall. *Bam.*

Inside is my little stash. The perfect stash. The stash that will unlock the doors to the realm I'm supposed to be in. Or at least get me a step closer to them.

The jar unscrews easily and I scoop a little powder and mix it into another bottle of water. Shaking it up, I'm bored. This feels so monotonous. It's the same thing I've done three times before and yet still, nothing.

That's what they say the definition of insanity is, isn't it? Doing the same thing over and over and expecting a different result?

I inspect the water bottle in my hand, watching the little fizzy bubbles make their way to the top. Pop pop pop. Little bits of air wanting to be carbonation. Yet, no matter how many times they show up and creep to the surface, they get the same result.

Pop pop pop. Insanity.

But I'm not insane. I know the difference between reality and possibility. Talent and hackery. This realm and the next. What's promised and what's due.

This stupid bottle. How many times have I seen it like this before? I'm starting to lose count.

"Need a drink?" I repeat. I think I repeat it, but again there's no real answer. Why do I have to work so hard for an answer when all it takes is yes? A nod. I'll even take a grunt or two.

Maybe I need a new clipping. My hand reaches into my back pocket again. No; there's enough there. But maybe I need a different clipping. Different clipping. Different result. Goodbye, adios insanity. Ha. Ha. Ha.

The thing on the floor twitches. Just enough to let me know it still has a semblance of life in it. Life that means nothing now. Again, I remind myself I can't have this here, where I'd have to lug it out or leave it. Where it'd be found and tied to me, my name, and prevent me from stepping into what's owed to me.

It moves just enough to let me know it can stand up. Even if I have to help support its weight and walk it like it's coming home from one of those drinking parties. At this time of night, everyone down — Deuces, they call it — would have embarrassing low control over their own bodily functions and movement.

It would fit right in.

I suck in a breath. "Alright, let's go."

A shallow breath response.

I can see it's not going to move without a little motivation. A nudge. A promise, maybe? So I bend down and lift an arm. I can feel the thing's muscles fight back.

"See, no big deal!"

And I pull it up. Even though it could fight me back more, it won't. I'm its last promise, after all. Last promise before it moves over to the next one or not.

So slowly it gets to its feet. I pull the thing to a straightened position. The movement must have been too much because everything from deep inside of it complains and convulses until the thing's mouth opens up and out spews everything. Everything that it ate since, well, I guess since this morning.

The sour smell hits the air, my clothes, and my nostrils hard. Assaults it, even. And I'm almost ready to wretch myself. But I realize that this?

This means two things. One, that my time is more limited than I even thought a few minutes ago. And two, that as long as we can make it to the outside world, then we are in the most perfect location possible.

No one would think differently.

The stairs will be the most difficult of the journey. Good thing they're first. Then this thing can use whatever strength is left to move its way up up up and into the promised land. Promise for it. Promise for me. Promise for us all, la dee da.

Each step feels like a mountain with the extra weight on my shoulders. But we make it. Well, I make it. I'm not sure the thing attached to me even notices a difference. It's moaning, though, so I know it'll still make movement when needed. When I ask. Encourage, and all that.

"Another step," I try my best. And it does it. Another foot goes up another mountain and before I know it, we're at the very top and I'm closer to my promise.

Promised land, promised promises.

And light. Day. Well, actually night.

It's night. But outside feels like a whole new day. In the darkness, we walk. I could sing a merry little tune if only… if only I could carry one. But I'm carrying too much already. Too much baggage, too much hope, too much of too much for one single man in one single night.

And the music here, it fills the air with its boom boom booms and thudity thuds. Every single person on this row, street, the deuces, whatever the name is these days, they're all inside. Behind the doors and windows and clouded by cloudy decisions no one should be making within those houses.

I stop. A single form. A body. A person is standing on the street. No. On the side of the street. And it's not standing. It's squatting. Then it's shaking. And the wind must have picked up a little because it wafts toward me and fills up my already soured nostrils.

This is why they call it deuces.

The person shakes a leg, literally, and pulls up its pants. Then, it parades inside one of the houses like a proud peacock who has just shown its prized feathers.

A stumble. A trip. A "hey now, we're almost there." And we're past the first Deuces house. The second. The smell strengthens and I see it. A pile of clay-colored crap right off the sidewalk.

"Step up and over." We make it. Nothing tracking at the bottom of these four shoes.

The sound of several voices wakes my ears and kickstarts a pounding in my heart. And I wonder who might be out here, watching the new deuces kid out in the open. Then I see a circle — no; not a circle — a ring of people in one of the yards. They stand side by side, shoulder to shoulder, then all step back in unison. They're speaking in some other language — Greek, probably — all in unison. As they step back again, their chanting gets louder. Their palms raise to the sky and touch together. Open palm to open palm, each person in the circle — no, the ring. This isn't a circle, *the* circle — tilts their necks back and aims their face to the sky.

Every face is hidden, covered by a dark hood.

My heart stops pounding. Even if one of these dark hooded people sees me with this thing, they're way too busy with their ring chanting to give me any notice.

Step by step, we move again. Past another house and another until we end up on a side street. A row of apartments full of people who loved to live here and lived to love here, in this small town of promised promises.

Behind them. In an alley. Just a few steps away from where she — no, it — could have come from, walked away from, and landed.

Plop. There it goes. To the ground. Slumped against a dumpster. Every family member in the apartments stacked up asleep and sound, resting up for a new morning.

Now that it's disposed of, done, goodbye, adios, I know what needs to be done.

I need to break the cycle of insanity. A new craft, a new lock, a new promise for the realm that's got a little nook carved out for me.

There is space in The Circle that's calling me, and one way or another, I'm going to claim it. Even if it means recruiting the one person who will ensure it while breaking my heart, I will have that spot.

CHAPTER THIRTEEN

The Melting Clock House

Every time my foot hits a new step, there's a new soft thud that sounds off in the air. And every time Livvy takes a step behind me, her nerves complain in an echo. I try to shush her, but I'm too focused on how shaky my feet are and how strong the smell of must hits my nose.

"Ugh, I hope no one died here." Livvy's voice is a mixture of jest and deep concern, and I can't help but wonder the exact same thing, especially after recent events. Why would there be a room underneath my washing machine? A room without a light fixture, without easy access, and that certainly wasn't included on the 900 square footage listing.

And with two bodies already scattered in the area.

Part of me wonders if I just scored extra space without paying for it. Another part of me is a thousand percent sure there's going to be a dead body at the end of the steps, rotting and waiting for me to trip over it, break my ankle, and die right in its spot.

I brace myself when my foot hits the cement under the last step, only slightly relieved there's no dead body in sight. A sweep of the flashlight, and I can see the bigger picture of the room we're in. It's big. Bigger than the kitchen it's under. And oddly, even though it seems like it would make for a great crawlspace, that's not what this is.

It's more like a half-finished basement. Cold, musty, but oddly, it's not damp. The atmosphere fills me with a concoction of creepy jitters and excited goosebumps. Like there are secrets down here waiting for me to unwrap them.

Awesome.

"Look at that!" Livvy's voice cuts through the darkness and a second later, a light flickers to life above us. "Huh."

I give her a little, "Huh," back, because that's exactly how to describe what's in front of us. It's not nearly as creepy as either of our imaginations was making it out to be. My feet take ginger steps around the perimeter of the room. The cinder block walls are painted an empty white, reminding me of sadder versions of the classrooms at Volga University. I trail along one corner to realize there is an alcove cut out. It's like a room unto its own, and it would probably work as its own little bomb shelter with the way it's built up.

Dust threatens to scratch at my eyes as I trace the next wall and peer up at the ceiling. There's no real roof, just boards of wood — rafters that hang above our heads.

Right in the center is a single lightbulb hanging by a single cord. It's the only light source in the room, but it's enough to see in here. Just enough to keep the focus right in front of you.

There is only one piece of furniture down here, and it's an old gas stove with a tiny counter space and a couple of shelves next to it. I step up to the burners and turn one of the knobs. There's a slight *tick tick tick tick* before a flame makes its presence known. Fantastic. it works. The fact that I just found an oddly placed working second stove in my house, causes my heart to flip a little flop.

"Livvy… this is perfect."

She sighs. "Perfect?" Her lip curls up and her dark eyes squint at me as if she's trying to read my mind.

"Sure. Well, with a little paint here, a couple of tables and folding chairs there. I think I could fit at least five or six easels down here. Enough to paint the number of canvases I'd need for the gallery Stark is pushing me to do." I'm already picturing a mural on the biggest wall that faces the staircase. And a few cheap folding tables to use as workspace. "That little alcove would be perfect for my ever-growing stash of supplies."

Livvy's face lights up. "Are you talking about turning this into your own art studio?"

"Well duh. Where else am I going to work on my paintings? I can't exactly take over your dorm space every time inspiration hits."

The idea of having enough pieces to apply to the art show would be a reality. And not just any regular pieces, but pieces that *actually meant something*. Like the Crane painting and the Andrea painting.

My heart gains seven pounds of emotion thinking about them.

And then my heart leaps for a little joy.

Because if I could actually have a space dedicated to doing this, reaching for the voices that couldn't speak up for themselves and telling their stories through acrylic and canvas, then I would prove to myself and my doubtful mother that I can actually make this a career.

College degree be damned.

This could really work.

"I was really hoping you'd keep some kind of statement piece in your new living room to scare away any weirdos you don't want hanging around too long."

"Eh. I let you hang around, and you're a weirdo yourself."

"Touche, friend." She hitches her eyebrow at me. "So…. is this your new project? A secret art lair?"

A snort of laughter erupts from me. "Sure, Batman. You ready to get this thing straightened up?"

"Nuh uh." She shakes her head. "This is *your* lair. That makes *you* Batman."

My eyes automatically roll themselves to the back of my head. "Okay, then, *Robin*, you gonna put your muscles to work and help me out?"

Livvy balls up her fist and flexes a bicep. It protrudes out as a surprise threat that I didn't even know was there. "Of course, I'll help," she tells me. "But it'll have to wait until the weekend. Art history is kicking my butt. I don't know why you wanted to major in it in the first place."

I shrug. "Well, it's not like the entire major is memorizing dates, names, and religious influences. You just have to do your time learning the boring stuff in order to get to the good fun stuff."

I take another look at the large blank wall facing the staircase. Anything could be there. Anything at all. The problem is, *anything* is too much of a possibility. It doesn't give me any direction. Even if I put my special paintbrushes to work, I don't think I'd know what to do with such a large blank space.

"Sure, this weekend," I tell her. "Come by on Saturday and we'll fix up this place together. I'll even let you take the space over there." I point toward the left of the basement. "Bring whatever you want. This is big enough for both of us, and I could use the company."

Livvy's face lights up, and she agrees. "Saturday. You've got it."

"And I guess in the meantime, I need to go visit Stark."

***

There's always a row of mixed and rejected half pint aluminum paint cans in the discount aisle at Craft Your Pants. The swatches on the lids are always smudged and scratched off to the point where it's impossible to tell what color and shade lives on the inside. But that's okay. Even when the swatches are still visible, it's not like the color actually matched well enough to them. That was the charm of these paints. Anything could be in them. And sometimes, the thrill of unknowing is just what I need. Sometimes, the mystery of what they are is where the best messages are found.

I scootch my cart close to the discount paint shelf and rub my hands together.

Who's coming home with me today?

"You, you, and you," I willy-nilly pick up three random cans. Reaching my hands on the shelf again, I pull a few more, just enough to make my basket feel well-fed. It doesn't matter if the inside is bright chartreuse or puke green. Part of the fun is challenging myself to come up with artwork based on the colors fate chooses for me.

And, heck, with a new secret basement art studio lair, anything is possible. Anything.

Anything. I really hope I can come up with something.

The familiar bright white smile catches my eye at the checkout. I don't care how many times I see Stark's face, I still feel a little nervous around him, even after I've seen him covered head to toe in dumpster juice.

"Hey, you." His voice is deep and smooth, and I feel like hiding behind my wireframe cart.

"Hey." I wave back. "What are you reading?"

He pulls out a white paperback from behind the register. The title, *History of Paintbrushes,* is front and center. The cover's border is decorated with several different brushes with wooden and plastic handles as well as all types of bristles. One even has feathers tied to the end in a little puff to paint with.

Okay, so I guess Stark is a nerd in his own way. But it doesn't make me any less nervous to be around his beaming smile and kind eyes.

"Nice." I nod. "Doing a little research?"

"I wanted to know more about that brush you showed me the other day."

"You mean, this one?" I pull one out of my back pocket to show him. "Or this one?" I pull out its auburn-haired twin.

"You've got another I see!" His eyes grow wide and so does his smile. He's as excited as I am, I think. "You know, the first brushes were made in the Stone Age?"

"I guess they had to paint their caves with something."

"Yup, and even though many brushes are mass-produced with wooden and plastic handles, some people still make their own by hand."

I nod and twirl the two brushes in my hand. "Sure seems like it."

"Usually, with handmade ones, artists like to use natural materials. Things like sturdy sticks from the ground and tufts of animal hair."

"Animal hair," I consider. And yeah, it does kind of look like animal hair. A fox maybe? Foxes come in different colors. They look nice and fluffy. I bet their fur is soft, too.

"Fox, mink, you know, pretty much anything like that."

"So, does your book tell you who in our little community might have made these?" I ask hopefully.

Stark shakes his head. "Sorry, Mills. I still don't have a clue about that." He tucks away his book for later and takes a look in the cart. "Ready to check out?"

I pull out two cans of paint, one in each hand, to put on the counter.

His eyes track each can as I place them in front of him, one by one.

"A new project, I see. There's nothing quite like starting up something brand new, not yet knowing what you'll come up with, huh?" He curls up one side of his lips and then adds, "Is it anything like the one we pulled out of the trash together?"

I can feel my face turning red. I'm sure I've turned into a tomato.

"You know, I've said it before and I'll say it again." He grabs one of the cans and scans it. "You have more talent in one hand than most of the people in this shop have in their entire DNA."

There's a familiar scoff behind me, and I can hardly believe it when I turn my head. The woman with the coke bottle glasses is standing behind me. Again. Ready to throw spit in all directions with her frustrations flying from her mouth.

I smile. Nod. Cross my fingers she doesn't remember me from before.

"You know, there are people out here. Real people who have worked themselves to death — literal death — to perfect their talents. You can't possibly tell me this *girl* has put in enough effort to match the talents of the people who are killing themselves for the sake of their art."

Yup. She remembers me. And she holds an even bigger grudge than I could ever imagine.

Stark holds his hand up to this woman, and in the calmest voice I have ever heard him use, he says, "Ma'am, I'll be with you in a second. I'm helping another customer right now."

Bam. Woman is shut down. She scoffs again and spittle — literal spittle — flies from her mouth when she does.

Batty woman.

Stark scans the last of the cans and hands it to me with a wink. "Is that all, miss?"

"Yup," I tell him, while I try to figure out how I'm going to balance my paint all the way home.

"Oh, but I don't think it is." He winks again.

"Here we go," the woman spits and one of her extra wide eyes behind her glasses twitches. "I can't wait to leave this realm."

Yup, definitely batty.

"Hold on right there." Stark nearly disappears behind the counter, crouched down and rummaging through the shelves out of my view. I have no idea if he's going to share another book with me or another flier, but what he actually pulls out is definitely not what I expected.

"A paintbrush!"

"A paintbrush."

I take it in my hands and run my fingers over the bumpy handle. I use my fingernails to inspect the bristles. They're a light brown, almost mousey, and move like liquid through my fingers. It's just like my other two, but different. Like sisters of a set.

"How did you get this? Stark! You're over here telling me about the history of the craft and you've been holding out on me?" I turn around, ready to bolt back to the paint section and do a little search and rescue mission to stockpile these magic brushes.

Stark gives me a deep chuckle. "No, Mills. You're not going to find any back on our shelves."

"Humpf."

He gives me a shrug and the crazy lady - yes, I said crazy, because that's what I'm deeming her now - lets out her own dissatisfied sound.

Stark continues to ignore her and I have zero doubt that she is contemplating whether or not to actually crap her pants, right here, just like the name of the store says, just to get noticed.

"I went on a five-minute break, just to step away when things were slow. I didn't even think anyone was here. Just stepped outside for some fresh air, and when I got back, it was here. Just laying on the counter." Stark hands it to me.

"It looks hand-crafted, doesn't it? It's definitely hand-crafted. Do you think the artist came by for supplies and accidently left it behind? Won't they want it back?"

Stark sucks in his bottom lip and knits his brows. "Nah. When I saw it, I called out to the store just to see if anyone was in here I didn't notice. Turns out, there was a man, and when I called to him, he walked out the front door and disappeared around the corner. My guess is he wanted to drop off a sample for us to test out on our own. If he's really interested, he'll come back and ask us if he can supply more for our shelves."

"So, are you going to test it out?"

Livvy-rumor has it that Stark was once an amazing artist but he sort of grew out of the practice years ago. I take a look at his dark hands, imagining how each of his digits may move in ways to conjure up images I've never created myself. I'd love to see what his hands could do.

"Nah. I thought you'd be perfect for the job." He puts his hands in his back pockets, showing me there is no way he is going to accept this paintbrush back.

It is mine now, to work beside my others.

I now have three brushes that could tell their stories together.

CHAPTER FOURTEEN

"Did you know that strawberries have more sets of DNA than bananas?"

"That's because strawberries taste better."

"So, are you hypothesizing that the more DNA something has, the better it tastes?"

I stop in mid-brushstroke to glare over at Livvy across the room. She's helped herself to a corner of my basement-lair to set up science shop, which beats sharing a dorm room with either Janelle or my former roommate who I never really took the time to get to know — or the rotating boys she brought back to sleep with at any given time of the day.

She glares back at me. Given the situation around town, dark humor probably wasn't the most appropriate. But, hey, it's us. And sometimes we have to let out a dark joke now and again to keep ourselves from falling into the shallow depths of despair.

And, yes, I called them shallow. It seems like we're always wading through them, and yet it doesn't take much to fall in and drift away. But if you have the right person by your side, you can climb out and get back to standing.

A few minutes of a mutual stare down and we both get back to our projects: her with whatever she's doing with fruit DNA and me with my mural.

I still don't know what it is, but now that I have three artisanal brushes with bristles softer than baby wool, I don't need to know. I just need to let my tools do their thing and I'll sit back to let the art happen. I'm sure whenever it shows its final face, I'll know what to do with it. I'll be able to hear its message loud and clear.

"And did you know that bananas share 50% of DNA with humans?" She questions me again. And I can't help to compare humans to the fruit I like the least.

"Well, I guess that means that humans aren't so tasty after all."

I stop again in mid brushstroke. I probably crossed a line there.

Livvy scoffs. "That's not exactly what I was talking about."

Line crossed or not, it's an opportunity for me to jump over it. "So, are we back to saying humans taste -"

"I'm saying nothing about cannibalism, Emily Ellis!" Livvy cuts me off at a sneer.

I do my best to push forward, keep going, and ignore the line that was now crossed twice by letting my painting take on more shape.

"I'm saying," she continues, "that it's interesting. The DNA of you or me or anyone else is so close to something as simple as a banana. And when we eat it?"

"Uh," I try to follow Livvy's thoughts, "does our DNA change every time we eat a fruit salad?"

"Nope, but it does have different effects on our bodies. Like, it'll aid in the synthesis of hemoglobin."

Another dip into cerulean blue and my brush dances against the cinder block, leaving a mark every step the bristles take to the beat of its own patterned rhythm.

"And I'm guessing it's good to have extra hemoglobin?"

"It is if you're anemic."

"No problem there, friend."

She shuts her laptop and crosses her arms, her hazel eyes narrowing at the wall in front of me. "So, what are you calling this piece?"

I make another few strokes, letting the brush do its thing. Once it feels like there are no more marks to make, I place the brush down on my table and step back.

"I don't think I have a name for it yet."

The wall is now covered in blues and reds and two shades of purple. Thanks to the magic of blind color selection, there was even a little unintended grey. But it works. The whole piece works. Abstract lines twist and turn around each other and circles overlap each other in a pattern somewhere between lucid and vague.

There's a message in here somewhere, I just don't know it yet.

"I think I'll call it…"

"Beans," Livvy states with utmost certainty.

"Beans?"

"I was just thinking, I wonder what kind of things beans do to your body when you eat them. Or if different beans do different things. Or if their DNA breaks down differently than you'd expect."

"Beans are just beans, Livvy."

"But are they? *Are they?*"

But then it hits me. This isn't just any 'ol abstract painting I've created. And it *does* have a story to it. In fact, it has a story that's still going on right now, as we speak. A story that is still bugging me with a heavy unresolve.

"Oh crap, Livvy."

She pushes herself from the table she's sitting at and makes her way over toward me. "What's wrong, Mills?"

"It's Volga." I point to my painting.

She scratches at the puff of hair on the top of her head. "Sorry. I don't get it."

"It's a map. It's a map of Volga, campus at all."

I dip my best brush into a little bit of black paint, and before the entire thing can dry, I make two circles.

One on campus. Malory Gibbons.

One on Deuces, frat row. Andrea Shepherd.

"Hey, Liv?"

"Yeah, Mills?"

"Do you remember the story of the girl from over the summer?"

Her face drops. "Yeah. School wasn't in session yet. But she was visiting or something. She wanted to test out the campus with a few friends and ended up getting lost on the streets."

My voice drops, too. "Yeah. They found her right down the road. Somewhere between here and campus, right?"

Livvy walks over to my mural map and points. "If this is the campus courtyard," she moves her finger over to another shape, "and this is us," she points right around where Joe's is, "then she was there. Hit by a car after she fell sick in the road." Her voice trails off, saddened by the memory of someone we could have met and never did.

I paint a third circle, for the summer girl.

And then Livvy's phone rings. "Hey, brother." As she listens to Stark on the other end, her entire energy shifts. No longer quiet and sad, she's stoic, holding her ground. Even though her eyes shoot open and I can see the bullets of fear within them, her voice doesn't have any sign of shaking. "Stark? Stark, calm down. Tell me again. What's going on?"

Livvy's fear bullets hit my heart when she repeats what she heard. "Another girl. Between Broad and Cumberland. Sam Aleah."

I make a fourth circle, between Broad and Cumberland with the face of the punchy girl from class. Sam Aleah.

"It's not just a map, Livvy. It's a murder map. Someone is murdering these girls, Livvy, and this is a map to track them."

CHAPTER FIFTEEN

The paint on my mural map is still sticky wet. The circles I made for each of the gone girls are glistening with paint. The fourth circle for Sam is dripping down the mural. It almost looks like the mural is crying dark tears. I want to as well.

Four. Four girls.

There is no way this is a coincidence. There's no way any food poisoning or alcohol poisoning or any other kind of poisoning has randomly found these girls to tick away their lives. This job has been carried out by someone's hands.

And if the police are keeping quiet, and the families aren't saying anything, who is going to share these girls' stories? Who's going to sniff them out, untangle the realities, and make sure the world hears them?

I slam my paintbrush on the table. Me. It's got to be me.

"You okay, Mills?" Livvy breaks her silence. The phone call from Stark has both of us stunned, shocked, and stuck in confusion.

"No. No; I'm not."

And I'm really not. Not too long ago I was so damn focused on painting a picture that told the story of a creepy professor on campus. But now, looking at the three circles on this mural-map, I realize how ridiculous that was. It's not about calling out a professor anymore. It's about using my voice when others can't use theirs.

I should have talked to Malory. I should have asked her what was going on.

Not that she would have told me a thing. But I could have at least tried to get to the truth of the matter. Attempts don't hurt when good intention is behind them.

But now I'm stuck listening for truths in the quiet of taken voices.

"I should have been more careful."

Livvy shakes her head. "None of this is your fault, Mills. You know that, right?"

"No." I shake my head back at her. "I mean, yes. I mean…" I think about my next words carefully. "Livvy, I should have been more careful with the Crane painting."

"Okay." She nods. "Maybe something a little less dramatic would have kept you on campus."

I frown. "It's not about being on campus. I don't care about that. It's that, you know how you say that you study science because of how honest it is?"

"Yeah." I can tell in her voice she's unsure of where I'm going with this.

"Well, that's why I love art so much, too."

"Okay…"

"Except science honesty and art honesty are a little different. Science honesty is all in the brain, in your head. And art honesty is in the heart."

Livvy bites her bottom lip as if she's digesting my words on an already full stomach.

"When you have a petri dish, microscope, and vials of who knows what in front of you, you come up with black-and-white answers. The proof is in front of you. The story is in front of you with all of its details. And no one can dispute how wrong it could be, because it's all there in front of you."

I swallow back a breath of air. "But in art? The honesty comes from the artist." And now it's my turn to bite my lip. "But when I painted Malory and Crane in that way… well, I was telling my story. Or rather, the version of it I thought was real." I pause and think about how it was different from the Andrea painting. "But even if it's what I thought was real, I should have told her story. Malory's story. And I didn't do that.

The Andrea painting, though, was outside of me completely. I saw what she saw. Not just what I think she saw, but what I *feel* she saw. I held that brush in my hands and I captured what came to me without thinking. And it became part of her story. Not some crazy gossip. No hearsay. Just what I feel is right."

"So, you want to tell the truth of what happened to these girls?"

I nod. "Yeah. But more than that, I want to get it right. I want to do them justice." I spin around to face Livvy. "Look, I'm not some crazy detective or anything. I'm no armchair sleuth. But I am an artist. So I can do something, right?"

It feels so heavy. And wrong. Sure, I could paint a few pictures, but would that even mean anything? Maybe it would if I could do more than speculate. Maybe if I could get some more information. Get a fuller story.

That's what scientists did, right? If they didn't have all the information they needed, then they'd do some more research, another test, mix a few new things together to understand it all better.

"Ugh, Livvy." I slip down to the cold floor and hug my knees tightly. There's a speck of blue on the concrete. It must have dripped from when I was painting, but the shade doesn't match exactly. I tap it with my thumb, but it's dry. It's as if it's been there for months.

"Have you ever questioned if you're doing the right thing with what you do? What you study?"

"Mills, I was just pulling apart the DNA of a strawberry. Of course I question it. I question it all the time, but then I remember why I do it. Sure, I might be studying fruit DNA now, but that's going to lead to human DNA, which will lead to curing diseases or creating medicine or who knows what." She shrugs her shoulders. "I think when you have a gift, it's natural to question the whys behind it. But eventually, it all makes sense. Eventually, I'll be in a lab somewhere helping create an antidote for poisons."

116

She crawls onto the floor next to me, right by the speck of blue. The blue that's looking less like the cerulean I was using and more like a bright, electric shade. "And, eventually, you're going to be in some big shot art show, and people are going to travel from all over the world to see your paintings. They'll be fighting over each other to buy them, so that your stories, and whoever's stories you paint will be told on their living room walls, making them think about what they're looking at and hearing the voices of those who are behind it."

I bite my lip. It tastes like salt and worry. "I hope you're right, Livvy."

"I'm always right, Mills."

She's not wrong.

***

Standing smack dab in between the streets of Broad and Cumberland, I realize how cramped this alley really is. I guess I would have never noticed this was a dead end, only one way in and one way out. I don't make it a habit of walking down alleyways down the streets I don't live on. And my house is a block down from here.

And now that I'm here, standing between brick buildings with fire escapes, but no escape for anyone who might have been chased down this way, I wonder even more what had happened to Sam before she ended up here.

Here, slumped next the large green trash bin where everyone and their mother tosses their daily garbage. And how the heck did no one see her for two days, *two days*, after the last Deuces party? I shuffle my feet over to the dumpster. I don't even have to take a deep breath; the stink hits me like a car. A mixture of week-old leftovers gone bad in the back of the fridge and moldy towels people got too tired of dealing with after too long.

It's gross.

But I walk next to it anyway. I want to take it in, the place where Sam was found. I want to feel out this space and what it was like for her to sit here, unmoving, her body just waiting for someone to find her.

So I crouch to the ground and imagine myself laying there, halfway propped up by trash bags full of who knows what. The bag next to me looks as good as any, so I reach my hand toward it and cringe. A quick prayer goes through my head that this isn't full of rotten banana peels and a kid's dead hamster.

Unwinding the stretchy headband — Malory's headband — from my wrist, I slip it over my head and use it to pin back the loose strands of hair from my face. There. Now I can concentrate. Now I can sit back and *feel* where Sam was. Really feel. I tilt my head back and rest it on the dumpster behind me. My eyes close and I breathe in the image of Sam. Tall. Mousey hair. Quiet the majority of the time with a mouth full of sass when she needs, and pearls on her ears.

Pearl earrings.

I dig out a small canvas from my bag and the bottles of paint. My hand grabs hold of my newest paintbrush and I let it go to work. It starts with Sam's caramel eyes, then moves to her nose, lips, and chin. The outline of her face appears in front of me the way it's showing up in memory. Her mouth gapes open, shocked at what she sees.

What does she see?

Maybe it's the fact that my hair is pulled back, or maybe I really am channeling my painted subject, but my hand moves to paint in a headband, pulling her hair back, too. Her clothes are disheveled. Her eyes are scared. Something in front of her scares her.

It's looming. It's shadowy.

I let my hand do the moving, my brush do the work. I don't think about Sam anymore because I don't have to. She's showing up in front of me the way she's supposed to, the way she's meant to, in order to tell her message.

And all of a sudden, her eyes are filled with more than fear. It's betrayal. Cream and vanilla paint works feverishly over her features, creating worry lines on her forehead and around her mouth.

The figure in front of her wasn't always scary. Her look says that at some point, she had trusted it. But now, it's looming over her, making her feel small, shrinking her confidence down to a speck.

I try hard to picture the figure, see what it is — who it is — but it's not clear. It's just a shadow. Blurry and dark. So, greys and blues come out to play. A blurred outline shows up and I swear I expect a profile with a hooked nose. A Crane nose. Because who else could put this betrayed fear on her face? That must be the connection, right? It's what I've convinced myself as truth.

But the nose doesn't hook.

And the hair is longer than expected.

My brush continues to move, making background strokes of whites and greys and... that's not the dumpster.

Why isn't she by the dumpster?

But I can't question that now. I can't stop, I can't refocus. The paint has a mind of its own, filling in the blanks until there is no blank canvas left.

The last brushstroke is quick, finalizing. And it's a single pearl earring. Sam is *The Girl with a Pearl Earring*. The girl with a pearl earring who has been betrayed by whoever that blurry figure belongs to.

Without the Crane nose.

And with long hair.

And I remember Sam meeting with Mariëtte. Who told her she'd be next. "You're next, Aleah!"

Mariëtte Dunn. I knew there was something off with that girl. The question is, what was Sam next in?

I look down at the painting I created. Maybe I already know that answer.

CHAPTER SIXTEEN

Him

I think I know what the problem is, though I'm not sure I want to admit it. In fact, I'm pretty sure the problem has been under my nose the entire time and I just hadn't willingly put my thumb on it yet. It took a few tries. A few trials that turned out to be erroneous errors.

Sweet, beautiful errors who had a leak of potential.

I wish I had been right about them. It would have made things easier. I don't really want to recruit her. She has more potential to be higher than a recruit. I'd much rather her stand in a mastery spot next to me. So we could go to the realm together, become masters together, watch this realm burn and live in the peace of the next realm together hand in hand as equals the entire way. That was my original plan, but plans change, don't they? Mine has to.

If it's going to be me or neither of us, it's going to be me.

If none of them provided me with what I needed, then they would have never measured up to be good enough recruits anyway. They all turned out to be *things* in the end. *Things* that used up all their usage even before they were possibilities. There's only one solution I can come up with. It's not the one I want, but it's the one that makes the most sense.

The most frustrating thing is knowing what I'm due and not having the key to open up the realm of possibility to myself. Everything I've tried so far, all the talent I attempted to extract hasn't been enough. I need *real* talent, something that isn't going to peter out at a single brushstroke. I need something that's actually going to push me over the edge, to a place where there's no return, no coming back from.

And that something has been at my reach all along. I just never reached out and grabbed it. All the testing has been done. I've provided her with tools to use with her own hands, and to my non-surprise, she's outperformed every one of them.

I'm sure she would deliciously outperform in every sense of the term, too.

This realm of possibility... Oh, how I imagine what it's like for people like me. It's a place where everyone knows everyone by exact name and aura, where we can all sit in a circle and praise the work of one another with open hands and open hearts. There's no competition or struggle to one-over anyone else. It's just, "You're the best, and I'm the best, and we'll be the best together. We'll all be mastery masters together."

It just makes sense that there's a place for me to stand in that circle. If only I could secure that spot.

There is a way. This bright yellow paper is my ticket to getting there. **Fine Art Auction** in bold typeface might as well say **Fast Pass to Mastery.** At least, it will be, as long as *she* will be there. And she will. I just need to ensure those canvases are in my possession. All that will take is a single call. That's it. Then she and I and they and it and all the mastery talent in the world will be in my hands, running through the tippy-tips of my fingers, and driving me straight to the vessel that will take me to the seat in the realm's circle where I belong.

I've seen her work. She has no business wasting her time in college, earning a degree she doesn't need. I'm so glad she's seen that, that she understands that. What can a person do with an arts degree anyway? Teach how to dip a brush into watercolors? Trust me, that's not a way to live out expertise. No one appreciates it. If she were prepped more, if she understood where she could possibly put her talents to use, she'd have a place for herself to be a master as well.

But she hasn't. She's been so wrapped up in her young hopefulness of becoming something with her education, she hasn't bothered to get an education of what really matters. I've learned a long time ago, nothing in this realm matters unless it can help you into the vessel that will take you to the next.

She's perfect for me, this thing. No; she's not a thing. Not yet. Hopefully not ever. I need to remember that. She is a perfect *being*. I have to keep her that way. She's perfectly perfect to grab hold of, take her talent, and use it to amplify who I am in the eyes of the dignitary.

She'll be my special tool to use. Even better than the ones I've crafted. Because she will actually become the key I need.

In just a little while, I'll be standing in the center, surrounded by the artwork of all these so-called talents. Young men and women with paint brushes and acrylic in their hands whose imagination runs wild for the world to see on canvas. They're so cutely hopeful.

I'm one hundred and seventy percent sure the rest of the recruits are going to be hacks compared to her. They'll all have pretty little scenes of flowers and mountains. Maybe little cherub faces frolicking in fields, some junk like that, that all the other hopefuls will think is enough. I don't care how technically perfect any of the other recruits may be in their skill, hers is the only one that will allow me to enter the other realm when the time comes. Quite possibly, I'll be the only one who will be gifted a spot with a bow tied on top. My recruit is going to blow every single one of those sweet paintings out of the water and into a black hole. I've made sure of that. I've provided her with the tools to do so.

It takes my breath away with what she can do with a simple paintbrush. But the special ones? Well, let's just say that they're next level. Next-realm level. A perfect nod to the classics mixed with the beautiful tragedies she feels she's witnessed.

Well, not exactly witnessed herself, but I've given her the gift of being a step closer to actually knowing the scenes she's painted. She does have this cute desire to make things right with her artwork. Calling out the baddies in her eyes and all that. Her intentions are so sweet, but the actual execution of those intentions with her color skill and interpretation is perfection. I can't wait to hold that perfection in my own arms. Feel it in its entirety. Consume it, consume her. And then sit in The Circle where I belong.

CHAPTER SEVENTEEN

Sometimes running my skateboard at night feels good. It feels like home. The fresh air clears my head, and I'm able to actually think straightforward thoughts:

Four girls have died in Volga.

They were probably murdered.

I need one more painting to submit to the art show.

The other three have been completed.

Crane is still creepy.

Greek life seems a lot like cult life.

Mariëtte knows something but isn't saying what it is.

Mariëtte.

The uneven sidewalk goes bumpbumpbumpbumpbump under the wheels of my skateboard as I think of her gorgeous blonde hair and that weird glare she always seems to give. I know sorority girls are strange in their own way, but she seems like a special kind of strange. A special big sister strange with a firm hand on her little sisters' every move.

I wonder what the sorority house looks like inside. I bet it's like the frat houses in layout and build, but has a scent of hairspray and peppermint schnapps instead of beer and vomit.

That's not fair. Sometimes jungle juice has a fruity scent to it. I can always sniff it out from my dilapidated front porch.

Deuces is oddly quiet tonight.

There's no one out in the open. No chanting or stomping or running circles on the lawns in the rain. There is no one out wearing Zeta blues or Beta green hoods. I don't even see any Alpha pinks.

So weird that you can color code these groups of people so easily.

Maybe the recent events have calmed this part of college life down a little. Only a few quiet lights flicker in the house windows. No loud music. No balking laughter echoing out into the air. No revolving door of frat brothers and sorority girls in and out of the buildings. No fruity jungle juice scenting the air.

It feels strange. Like a small ghost street void of anything resembling life. My foot pushes off the pavement and I roll faster down the street. I want to avoid this eerie feeling and get straight to campus, where there's bound to be some semblance of life.

The streetlights in front of me are a welcoming beacon. Volga campus in all its glory and high-rise buildings. Nearly every window is a square of yellow light, some of which include the outlines of students watching television or sitting at their desks. It's what I used to call home what seems like a decade ago.

But it's only been a few weeks.

Chattering laughter comes from the dining hall. I guess the kitchen stayed open late tonight. Exams are soon and staff members want to make sure even those who stay up past ten at night still get a good meal in.

A full stomach makes a full brain. At least that's what the signs would say on the dining hall's walls.

My wheels turn, and I'm off in another direction. Toward the gym. I can hear a few voices and I pray it has nothing to do with Crane. His is the last face I want to see, because I'm pretty sure I'll end up throwing literal punches if I run into him.

But it's not Crane. Can't be. Those are female voices. And even on Crane's most annoyed days, his voice didn't rise to this timbre.

"No way. Did you see the way he moved like that?"

"Yeah. That was pretty amazing! I didn't know an old man could be in such great shape."

"He's in great shape and knows exactly what he's doing."

"You're telling me! His body moves like a sphinx. I can't wait until I can move in the same ways."

Old man? Doing what kind of movements now? Oh gross. Maybe it is about Crane.

"He's not so old, you know. He's just, mature is all. And with maturity comes ability."

And now the old professor, the one with the wrinkles that outlined his crooked nose *isn't old*?

I mean, who knows. He could be somewhere in his… late thirties? I'm a terrible judge of age. Regardless, he's *old* compared to his students. And he's *too old* to be showing off how his body moves in whatever way they're talking about. Again, gross.

"Whatever. I'm just glad he was able to meet us privately. It was about time we got a few good minutes in."

There's a pause, a giggle, and then, "Yeah. My body is so sore after all of that. It's going to take me a few days to recover from everything he put us through."

"You get used to it. After a while, it doesn't hurt anymore."

And all of a sudden, one of the voices sounds familiar.

Bump. Bump. Bump. My wheels slow down as I approach the sound until I stop completely. I was right. That sound is coming from the blonde hair, blue-eyed Mariëtte Dunn. She's talking to a girl I haven't met before. Another Alpha pink girl.

After a couple more giggles, the second girl sighs and rubs her neck again. I can smell the sweat off of both of them, and her face looks particularly flush.

I meet her eyes, and she casts hers down. "I've gotta go, Mariëtte. I'll see you tomorrow?"

"Don't forget," Mariëtte tells her. And then she twists her fingers through a piece of the pink girl's loose hair. "I need yours, too."

The pink girl nods. "Yeah. No problem. Tomorrow, right?"

"Tomorrow." Mariëtte pats her handbag as if she's holding onto a delicate treasure inside.

They wave goodbye to each other, and I'm left standing in front of the Big Sister on campus, herself, watching her watch this other Alpha pink girl with an odd grin on her face.

I steal a glimpse at the campus gym. There's a single light on, and it's flickering eerily. Even though I've never been inside of it, I'm pretty sure that's Crane's office.

I've never had the *pleasure* of being called back there myself. There's only one reason I imagine he might be calling these two out in the middle of the night. For a *private session*.

"I should have brought that painting back to campus."

Crap. Did I just say that out loud?

The look on Mariëtte's face tells me I did.

"Hey, you're that girl, aren't you?"

And now I've invited myself into a conversation I'm not sure I'm ready to have.

"You are." She points a well-manicured finger at me. Fireball red. Nice choice deviating from Alpha pink. "You're that girl who painted that picture of Professor Crane and displayed it on campus."

Yup. Not only am I in the conversation, but she's gonna push me in the center of it. *Deep breath, Mills. Don't go pissing off the catty girl who is probably sleeping with the professor you hate.*

"I am that girl. And it was right there." I point behind her, right under Crane's window. "It's too bad no one appreciates good art, though."

Mariëtte puts her hand on her hip and sucks in her cheeks.

I kick my skateboard up and hold the edge of it in the palm of my hand.

It's the start of a standoff. I can't take back what I've said and nor do I actually want to. No backing down now.

"Good art?

"*Great* art."

"I wouldn't call that *thing* great."

"That *thing* took more talent than you have in your pinky."

"That *thing* was gross. And you know nothing of what talent I might have."

"You're right. I don't. All I know about you is that you spend your time yelling orders at girls who look like mini versions of you."

"You don't know the first thing about me or my girls."

"I know that they look up to you. And I know that they're willing to let you in on their secrets. And I know that you don't care at all when they do. All you do is laugh at them and tear them down when all they want is someone to listen to them."

"What the hell are you talking about?"

"I'm talking about Malory."

And that shuts her up. Good. Let her think about Malory for a minute. Let her think about the girl who wanted to be an Alpha being dead. Let her think about what her role was just days before her body was found by the dumpster.

"I-" Her voice cracks and her hand leaves her hip.

"Exactly. I heard what you told her."

"You don't know what you heard."

"It's not like you were being discrete or anything."

She cocks her head to the side. If I didn't know any better, I'd think she's confused by what I'm saying. But I do know better, and playing dumb won't work on me.

"At Joe's. I heard you and Malory. I should have stepped in. With the way she looked. She wanted your help and all you did was shoot her down."

She purses her lips in understanding. Good; let her recall that conversation in detail. "I didn't say anything that was - "

"Was he a gentleman, at least?"

She looks at me with furrowed brows. "Was who a gentleman?"

"You tell me." I swing my board up and point the front of it at Crane's flickering light.

"What are you talking about?"

A deep breath isn't enough to calm me down, so I huff out the breath I did take and bite my lip.

Mills, you don't have to be a sarcastic ass.

"*What are you talking about?*" I mimic her in a high-pitched voice.

Well, that was mature.

I take another breath when she curls up her lip at me.

"You were talking about Crane and Malory," I take a pause, "well, you know."

Her eyes widen, and her face turns redder than it already was.

"You don't know what you're talking about," she hisses.

"I absolutely know what I'm talking about," I hiss back. "I heard the two of you loud and clear. And that painting?" I slam down my board in the grass. "That painting was to tell the whole campus the same thing. Professors shouldn't feel the need to knock boots with their students."

"Knock...Boots?" Mariëtte laughs. "Who uses that phrase anymore?"

This is so frustrating. "The horizontal tango. The hanky panky. Shaking sheet. Bam bam in the ham."

That last one does her in. And as my face grows hot with frustration, hers grows red with laughter.

"I have never," she cackles, "in my life," she breaks for a breath, "heard such ridiculousness!"

Both of her hands shoot to her knees and she bends in half with amusement. As she does, the bag she had been holding slips down her arm and onto the ground. Mariëtte doesn't even notice she's cackling so hard, and the bag's opening widens just enough for a little plastic bag to fall out.

Odd. I would have thought something a little prissier would have come out of the little handbag, a lipstick or nail polish, something like that. But there it is, a little plastic bag that popped out of the purse and landed a few inches away from my feet.

I pick it up, unsure if what I'm seeing is right. It can't be, can it? With a little shake, the contents inside shift and move, sliding around across each other like a thousand soft bristles from a paintbrush.

Within seconds, all laughter stops, and I can feel the heat from Mariëtte's gaze burn into me. "Give that back." Her tone is dark, threatening.

But my ears ignore her. Because it dawns on me why the bristles of my brushes are so unique and why they can't be mass-produced by a machine to be sold in a store anywhere.

The bristles of my brushes look just like this. Little clumps of -

"Give. It. Back."

"Mariëtte," I ask, "why do you have a bag full of clumps of hair?"

CHAPTER EIGHTEEN

"Ouch!"

Mariëtte snatches the bag out of my hand, and in a naturally swift move, she scoops her purse off the ground, shoves the plastic bag inside, and swings the whole thing over her shoulder.

She scowls. "That isn't yours."

Of course it isn't mine. I don't have a reason to carry a bag of other people's hair in my purse. But why the heck is she?

"Why do you-"

"Back off," she cuts me off and storms her feet away.

Nuh-uh. She is not going to run away from me. Not when I just caught her red-handed with something that could possibly tie all the things happening in Volga together.

"Mariëtte, stop!" I make my way after her.

As she picks up her pace, so do I.

"Stop!" I yell when her feet quicken even more.

Pretty soon, we're both at a jog. Our feet quicken to a run, and before my eyes, she bolts into a sprint.

Without even realizing it, we pass the dining hall, the science building, and end up crossing over to the quad in front of the art department. This is where I used to spend my time. This is where I refined my love for painting. This is where I learned how to hone my talent and use it to communicate visually to the outside world.

Everything around us is illuminated by campus streetlights. It's somewhere between dark enough to get lost and light enough to find your way, which is kind of how I feel running through campus like this.

It's ridiculous, really, running after the pinkest of pink girls because she has a bag full of hair.

She's huffing her breath ahead of me at a crazy fast pace and my feet are thumping along the ground while my board stays under my arm. How are her legs so strong? Mine are already burning. Note to self: try running once in a while. It might do you some good.

Duh. My board. I guess I was so focused I forgot I was holding it under my arm this entire time. Another note to self: Get some sleep. It'll probably help keep your focus more. My board slams the ground and I catch up, rolling slightly ahead of her. I stop, step off, and address her face-to-face.

"Why do you have that?"

Her mouth hangs open, and she slightly pants. Like a little poodle who just ran laps around the yard only to be caught.

"You don't need to know."

Bull. I want to tell her about my paintbrushes. How they've mysteriously shown up in my possession. How each one has felt special from the moment I got it.

And how at the end of each wooden handle were bristles unlike any other.

Hair bristles.

And Sam. What did she mean by Sam was next? I needed to know what she meant by that, too.

Then it dawns on me. Oh no. My stomach ties in knots I can't untangle. Is Sam's hair in there? Malory's? Whose heads did these tufts come from?

I don't know how I didn't see it before. I don't know how it completely mystified me. Of course, I couldn't find these brushes in the craft store. They weren't made of nylon and polyester. They were made of hair. Human hair.

Creepy crawly shivers run under my skin, tightening those knots.

"Mariëtte, tell me. I need to know." My voice is as serious as it can get. I need her to answer me.

She shakes her head in quick, rapid motions. "No, you absolutely do not."

"Yes, I absolutely do." I take a step closer to her. And even though she towers over me by at least five inches, I stand my ground. Backing down isn't an option. I can't just walk away from the girl who has a bag full of hair that possibly made the hair-brushes I've been using as if that's no big deal. "It's important."

She scrunches up her face. Her two eyes squint into tiny slits. "Why on earth would that be important to you?"

Oh, I don't know. Maybe because I've been painting with *someone's hair* for the past few months. Maybe because these hair-brushes not so randomly landed in my lap and each one has helped me paint dead girl images. Maybe, just maybe, because my fear is telling me that each of my brushes holds the hair of the dead girls, and I need to know how real that could possibly be.

"Look, I'm not sure how to tell you this...," I take pause and chew on the inside of my cheek because I really don't know how to say it. It sounds crazy, doesn't it? To ask her if she's behind my drawer full of special paintbrushes made of human hair.

It sounds demented. But before I can even get a word out to try and explain it, she starts at me again.

"Listen, this," she pats the outside of her purse, "and anything in it has nothing to do with you."

"But it does-"

"And that back there," she points to the campus gym behind us, "as wrong as you are about all that, it also has nothing to do with you."

"Wrong? What do you mean?"

"No one is having sex with Professor Crane."

Excuse me, what did she just say? There's no way I heard her right. "Wait, what do you mean no one?"

"Well, I don't know what the man does in his off-campus hours, but with the amount of time he stays after to help, I don't know he'd have the time for it anyway. Not that I even want to think about that." She shrugs.

"So the conversation I overheard with you and Malory in Joe's…?" I let the question dangle, hoping she'll fill it in. Because, clearly, I haven't filled it in correctly myself. And if I don't ask to get it cleared up, none of this will ever make sense.

Her face hardens for a moment. "First of all, you shouldn't be sticking your nose into other people's conversations like that." But then her features soften. "Secondly, Malory had a hard time getting used to -" She pauses, tilts her head back, contemplating her next words. "She had a hard time getting used to the possibility of sorority life."

I kick the side of my board. "Mariëtte, I'm not going to even pretend like I understand what that means."

"It means that Alphas have a certain way of life, a certain standard, and we stand by it."

I think about the hooded robes. The matching pink shirts. The marching on campus, and Mariëtte's voice ringing in my ears as I overhear her commanding each girl to take whatever move she was orchestrating. I'd say they have a *certain* way of life.

"And sometimes," she says, "some girls just don't adjust well to it."

"And Malory was one of those girls?" Maybe Malory didn't realize joining a sorority would take up her time with matching sweatshirts and forced chanting. Maybe the more she learned about the Alphas, the more she found out how cult-like they were.

"Malory was… soft," she decides. But her voice sounds soft, too. She's not judging her potential sister with disdain. Instead, there's a hint of sadness, almost pitty. She misses her. "And no matter what I had told her, how much I encouraged her, she stayed just as soft."

"And what about Sam?"

She cocks her head to the side. "You mean Sam Aleah?"

"The one and only." I roll my eyes. "You said she was next. What did you mean?" Hearing her voice sadden makes me drop my guard, too.

"She wants to rush this year, but we were all full up, done with all of that. We can't take any more girls this year. She's up for next year. I nearly promised her a spot. Just like I did with Malory."

It doesn't surpass me that she's speaking about Sam in the present tense. I don't know how else to break it to her, so I swallow, look her in the eye, and just tell her, "Mariëtte, Sam's gone."

She knits her eyebrows together. "I don't understand."

"I mean, they found her body. Behind Cumberland, in the alleyway by the townhouses."

"What?" Her voice lowers to barely a whisper, "She wasn't strong enough yet, either."

"Mariëtte, I'm so sorry."

Whatever she's trying to tell me doesn't make complete sense. It's clearly a secret for the Alphas only. For the Greeks. And as creepy and cult-like as they might appear to be from my outsider's view, there's something in her thin voice, in her shaking chin, and the way her eyes are focused on nothing at all as if the only thing they can grab on to is the past she can't hold onto anymore. All of this tells me she's not as scary or mysterious as she has always seemed to be at all. She's just a girl who lost a friend. Two friends. That's it.

Whatever the creepy hair is in her bag, and whatever Malory couldn't handle, is irrelevant.

"I tried." Her eyes gloss over with tears. "I really really tried. I want the best for these girls, you know?"

I nod my head. I don't really know all the nuances to this, but I get it. She has more heart than she shows on the outside.

"That's why we were out here tonight. And, to be honest, why I'm out here every night."

The dam she's keeping up is about to break wide open. I nod again, encouraging it to.

Her eyes leak out a couple of tears that stick to her nose until she wipes them with the back of her hand. "But Malory was always tired. She said she felt like we were pushing her too much, too hard, too fast. Sam never even had a chance. I wasn't even able to help her."

Another tear rolls to her chin and she swipes it away. "But it wasn't enough. I shouldn't have let her walk away without being pushed even harder, relentlessly, even. I should have done more for her. Maybe then whatever happened to her wouldn't have happened."

What had happened to her. "Mariëtte, what did happen to Malory?" I still didn't know any more than the rumors that didn't make sense.

"Some kind of drug that someone put in her drink." She rolls her eyes. "Or, at least, that's what they said. I don't think it's that simple. I think it's something much darker than that. I don't think this was some stupid frat party thing that went wrong." She stops to collect her shaking breath. "Sure, the boys there roughhouse, they talk big and all that, but they're not evil. Not that I've seen anyway. They're just stupid boys. Someone really wanted to hurt her. I just don't know why."

By now, her cheeks are wet and her nose is running. There's no distinguishing between snot and tears. It's all mixed up on poor Mariëtte's glistening face.

"That's exactly what I've been thinking, too. If someone wanted to hurt Malory," I ask, "then someone wanted to hurt all of them."

"All of them," she echoes. She's nodding in quiet agreement, like she's trying to make sense of what I just said, too.

"Mariëtte," I ask, "why do you think you could have stopped anything from happening? What were you doing with the pink-" I catch myself before I say something that might be offensive. "I mean, what were you and the Alphas doing that might have stopped something from happening? This isn't your fault."

"Because." She sniffles and digs into her purse. She must push the plastic bag off to the side because that doesn't fall out. Instead, she pulls out a wad of clothes that stink like Deuces. "Because we've been training self-defense with Crane."

Self. Defense.

And all of a sudden my stomach feels sick, like I could hurl up whatever might have been left in it from the microwaved mac and cheese I had earlier in the day.

Self-defense.

Crane had been meeting with girls. In his office. With Mariëtte and Malory and the pink Alpha girls who were wanting a little helping hand to keep themselves safe.

Maybe Crane isn't so creepy after all. Maybe he is just an awkward gym instructor who really is hoping to get his students in good shape, especially those who might need it on a college campus.

Maybe I should apologize to Crane. Maybe I should make it up to him somehow.

"Oh, and this?" Mariëtte breaks my thoughts, holding up the plastic bag in her hand. "It's stupid, really. And in light of everything else going on, there's no reason to keep some stupid sorority tradition from you." She shakes the bag in front of me and with her other hand, she wipes her face clean again. "Every Spring, we collect a small clipping from each of the girls. Then, before Summer hits, we burn them in a bonfire."

"Well, that sounds a little cultish." I can't help it. It does sound cultish.

She shrugs. "It's just a symbol of our collective. We might part in the summer, but there's still a part of each of us that's together."

I bend down and pick up the bag. For the second time tonight, I'm holding a bag full of hair. Only now, it's harmless, meaningless, just a silly thing the Alphas do. I hand it over to her. "By burning it in the name of the collective, you're not really helping your cult-case, you know." I smile and hope she can hear that I'm joking behind my words.

"Yeah. I've been told that before." She smiles back and moves the hair bag in her palm back and forth. "But why were you so hard-pressed to know why I have it?"

I shove my hand in my back pocket and retrieve a wooden handle. "Because, somehow, I've been collecting these, and I have no idea where they're coming from."

She takes the brush from my hand and flips it over so the bristles are standing up toward her. Waving it back and forth, her eyes follow the bristles' movement. They float and flutter as they move back and forth, silky-like and smooth. Like freshly conditioned hair.

"I don't know where this came from," she says, "but this isn't from an Alpha. This isn't from one of my girls."

CHAPTER NINETEEN

"Whoa. No way, Mills. I still don't know about this sorority stuff. No matter how innocent it all is, burning each others' hair in a bonfire is pretty damn cultish."

That's exactly what I said.

Livvy's voice over the phone is the reassurance I need to know that I wasn't crazy for thinking something was up with them in the first place.

"But you're right. And so is that Alpha girl. Something is happening to these girls. I didn't want to believe it, but you can't deny patterns, and there's a definite pattern here that is more than just suspicious."

And, her voice is the reassurance that I wasn't insane for thinking that something much crazier was going on with each and every girl they've found lining Deuces.

"The only problem is, if it really is poisoning, I can't see where that might be coming from. But you know, I'm working on it. Ever since I've sat down with fruit DNA, I haven't stopped thinking about what might cause a change in human health, or possible death. It could be the tiniest thing."

"Thanks, Livvy. I appreciate you."

"I'm just sorry I didn't see it before."

"I'm just sorry I thought my paint brushes were some kind of creepy serial killer trophy collection." With one brush in hand, I flick it back and forth on the table a few times. It rolls to the left a little, then right, then it hits my coffee cup with a *ping*.

The bristles really do look like hair. But that's not so abnormal, right? Stark's book even said that a lot of handmade brushes are made with animal hair. This is probably from some kind squirrel or a weasel. Any backyard hunter would be able to get ahold of that without any problem, sell it off to some local or visiting artist, and bam, out pops these amazing brushes that really are far better than the synthetic fibers at the local store.

"Maybe I need to just focus on getting these paintings done. You know, finish up this collection so there's enough for the gallery."

"There's only one left, right?"

"Yup."

"Then it shouldn't be a big problem, right? You've been able to get the others done in what? A couple hours?"

"Yeah, I guess so."

"So, get your butt out of Joe's coffee shop, go home, go downstairs into that creepy ass basement of yours, and get to work."

"Aye aye, captain."

"Look, I'm not the one who told you to get out and move into some crumbling house while you try to get on your feet. That was you. I'm just here to cheer you on and push you forward so that it gets done. I can't have my best friend just not finish something she said she was going to start."

"Yes. I get it, Liv." The paintbrush feels heavy in my hand, like the weight of my future has been injected into the handle itself. I shove it back into my pocket where it belongs for now. I'll drink my coffee, go home, and figure out how to round off this collection. "But it's not just about getting it done, Livvy. It's about making sure these girls' stories don't get drowned out. There's more to them than being the dead girls in Volga."

"I get it, too, Mills. There is more. And I feel like it's so close before we figure out what that more is." I can hear chatter of students who must be passing by Livvy. "Look, I'm almost to the chemistry building for class. Promise, I'll look into what I can over here. You just focus on your work. Paint for those girls and paint for yourself. But also for me. I don't wanna be without a friend in this lousy small town." She

141

pauses and clears her throat, then quickly says, "And neither does Stark."

I hear the audible absence of sound. Livvy's hung up, and I'm left with my thoughts, my cup of Joe, and a little bit of uncertainty in this crowded coffee shop.

College kids, professors, townies, and whatever the heck I'm now considered fill each fold out chair as if we are all attending some kind of kumbaya lawn party. Except, we're inside four unpainted walls at tables that are glorified TV trays, and we're listening to a local band's recorded album playing over the speakers. They're singing about tractor trailers and overalls, which you would expect would make them a country group. They're not. They're ska. And the contrast between their melody and lyrics rattle my brain even more than it already is.

My seat is a window seat, so I get the pleasure of enjoying the scenery - cars traveling fifteen miles per hour, drivers perusing the store fronts from the comfort of their vehicles. Once in a while, one eases into a parallel space to get a custom t-shirt made or browse the used book store. Maybe people watching is where I'll summon a muse for my next canvas. Maybe there's a story in one of these passersby, which is just as important as any of the others sitting in my basement.

My black coffee is hot, so I blow the steam away, and as I test the temperature with a sip, I hear my name.

"Miss Ellis."

I do my best not to spill my scolding hot beverage all over my arms by bracing my body not to jump at the sound.

"Sorry. I didn't mean to startle you."

My muscles ease as it registers. It's Noland. Without thinking, I offer an open hand to the seat across from me. It would be nice to be able to talk to the man who helped me tune into my inspiration in class. Maybe he could pull the same kind of inspiration out of me in the real world, too.

"It's okay," I tell him. "I was just people watching."

"Ah, a favorite pastime of many people, myself included."

His coffee smells sweet and sticky. It makes my stomach knot up. I don't know how anyone drinks their coffee drowning in sugar.

"Is this...weird?" he asks. "I can go, if it's weird to have coffee with an ex-professor."

I lean back in my chair and watch his thumbs caress his coffee cup. "No; not weird at all. I'm sure we've shared a table at Joe's before. Bound to with the way it fills up midday when everyone wants a little jolt of caffeine. No reason why this would be different."

"Oh it's definitely different. We don't have any projects to discuss."

A laugh escapes my lips. "Actually, I do."

His eyes widen. "So you're still putting yourself to work? That's great news!"

"Yeah. I heard about this thing I kinda want to do."

"Say no more," Noland reaches into his jacket pocket and pulls out a yellow piece of paper. It's an exact copy of the one I have back at home, waiting for me on top of one of my cheap tables. "The gallery, right?"

I nod. "Yup. So you know about it, too, huh?"

"Miss Ellis, you don't become one of the top art professors in a small town and not know about one of the biggest art events in the state. Of course I know about it. In fact, I was hoping you would apply. You have fantastic talent, and it would be a shame not to put it on display."

He leans back in his chair and for a moment, we're mirror imaging each other. Two people, coffee in hand, resting their backs on their chairs, easing into the effortless conversation we've always had, only with an entirely different vibe behind it.

We're no longer professor and student. He no longer has to give a crap about what I do. Yet, here he is, still encouraging me to do the thing I want to do. Better yet, it seems like he came here with the intention of encouraging me, even before knowing if I was interested or not.

"It's just that, well, I still have one more blank canvas I need to fill, and considering what I've done so far," painting the images of dead girls and what I think they might have seen, "I don't exactly know what to paint next." It's not like I can wish another body into the picture. I definitely don't want that. The entire point is that I don't want anyone else hurt. I just want to give them a voice.

It's not like I know much about the fourth girl on my list. In fact, as far as I know, it was just a freak accident. Since it was spread out months before the others happened, there's a high likelihood that her death and the others aren't even related. I'm not sure I'll be able to hone in…whatever it is I've honed in with the other three… with her, too. I'm doubtful I'll be able to hear her voice at all.

"Ah," he exhales loudly, and frowns. "Isn't submission due by the end of this week?"

I frown, too. "Yeah; just a few days. I sort of found out about this a little last minute, and now I'm sort of freaking out about needing to get it down fast and quick. And, well, I'm not so sure I can also get something done *well* in that time, too." As much as the stories of the girls in Volga are weighing on me, it's also weighing me down to think I won't even be able to participate in this mega-event that might keep me on my feet as an actual, factual artist.

His frown softens. "I see. If I remember correctly, you never had an issue whipping out some of the most uniquely satisfying pieces of art before. I'm sure you'll come up with something."

"Well, I always had to. For grades and stuff. Guess I got on a roll with creating and never stopped until-"

Noland barks out a laugh and his dark hair drops in front of his eyes. "Until that last doozy of yours."

"It was pretty brilliant, wasn't it?"

144

"I can't say that Professor Crane felt the same way."

I give Noland a smile. Of course, he gets it. He was the one who taught me that art needs to make a statement. That's what real artwork does. It makes you think. It makes you ponder about relationships and life. It reflects our actions and evokes our feelings. If it doesn't do any of that, it's not real art at all. It's just arts and crafts.

"I was wrong in painting that." My heavy confession doesn't lift, even when I say it out loud.

"Is that regret I hear in your voice, Miss Ellis?"

"I should have, I don't know. I should have asked more questions, listened a little better, you know, given the man a chance instead of just reacting with something so... jarring."

"You mean you should have put your talent on hold?"

"Noland! He didn't do it. He never touched anyone like I thought he did. You're not saying what I did was right, are you? You're not going back on what you originally said, right?"

"Well, maybe not exactly right. It certainly wasn't great for Professor Crane. But now that I don't have to tiptoe around your student duties, I can be blunt. When you feel like your hand and your brush have to move together, then you've gotta do it, right? Even you've said it before. Art creates itself. If you get that tingling feeling in your hands, it just means that the art is ready to be seen. You don't get a choice at that point. You just have to paint."

"Well, maybe I should have questioned that instinct a little, too. You know, waited until I knew for sure what was going on, and then I would have had a better concept to paint."

"Or you would have waited too long and then nothing would have come to you at all. Did you think about that?"

No, I hadn't thought about that, and I suppose he has a point there.

"Look, I have to admit, I was a little disappointed when I first saw what you did on campus. But not because of the content. It was because the second I saw it, I knew you'd end up fighting the system or something crazy like that and end up out of school. I was afraid you'd give up; stop painting altogether."

The look he had on his face is very clear in my memory. The disappointment was hard to handle, but I didn't realize it was because he thought I'd leave both campus and art behind. I figured he was like everyone else on that campus, sickened by the topic at hand and wishing I had never questioned such an upstanding professor.

Boy, do I get that now. I've jumped to far too many conclusions.

"Mills, if I were you, I'd put that painting in the past for now. Go grab yourself a blank canvas and just let your ambition do the rest. It'll come, promise. It has to."

"Yeah, I guess so."

He gives me a nod, then leans forward. I can smell the sugar on his breath. "Sounds like you need to clear your head." Then he puts his hand flat on the table and taps his pointer finger a few times. "Want to know what I do when I need to clear mine?"

Drink a bottle of gin? Go for a run? Call up some Craig's List Mistress? I couldn't imagine.

I stare at him. His dark eyes sparkle and the corners crinkle up.

"I clean."

Well, I didn't expect that.

"Like, your bathroom or something?"

He gives me a little shrug, but his eyes are still sparkling. "Sometimes the bathroom. Sometimes the kitchen. But when it comes to art, it's usually my brushes."

A chuckle escapes my mouth, "Yeah, I guess I can try that. Just need to dig up some castor beans or something to make sure they're done right." I know I sound sarcastic. Sometimes I just can't hold that part of me back.

146

Then I realize, Noland has only given me one of the brushes. He has no idea that more have dropped into my hands. "Oh, that's right, I haven't told you. I have a couple of new brushes. Just like the one you gave me that day in class. And you're right about them. There's nothing quite like them. They've been a major help in doing what I've already done."

Noland's coffee has cooled down enough for him to take a larger gulp from his cup.

That means mine has cooled down enough, too. So I purse my lips and my cup meets them. A long pull from my coffee fills me up with warmth and caffeine. The perfect combination.

A long, "Ahhh," spills from his mouth after his own drink, and then he says, "I guess that means you really do need a deep cleaning, then. Don't you?" Noland reaches into his jacket pocket and pulls out a small jar of oil. "Go ahead and skip all the sciency steps. Use this and get back to work."

The jar is cold in my hand. And heavy. And it's perfect. "Thanks, Noland. I'll bring this back to the house and try it out. I'm sure I'll come up with something."

"And if all else fails, paint yourself."

"Myself?"

"There's no subject you know better than yourself. I'm sure a self-portrait would be the absolute best way to round up your submission. I know I'd appreciate it as part of your entry."

Myself. A collection of dead girls and myself. I think I can do that.

CHAPTER TWENTY

I ease open the plastic drawer that serves as a paintbrush holder and pull out each of my unique brushes into tiny a row. All three of them look like sisters of an incomplete set, each with a slightly different handle with bumps and bends that give them their own unique shape. They started with Noland and ended with Kyle. And now I'm faced with the decision of how to put them to work to create the last painting I need to enter the art show, display my work, and let these girls' voices take over Volga County.

The last painting. What the hell should my subject be for my last painting?

I know Noland said I should do a self-portrait, and maybe I could. Maybe I should. Maybe there's a story of my own I need to tell.

But in comparison to the poor girls who have been taken away, nothing I can think of shines a light on the things that need to be told on their behalf.

The little jar of castor oil sits next to the line of brushes. Clear, goldeny liquid just waiting for something to take a dip in it, swim around, and leave satisfied and clean. I suppose that's why Noland had said he cleans, right? It gave him the satisfaction and focus to clean. Cleanliness equals clarity, and taking care of my brushes might just do the trick. It might just unlock whatever it is I'm supposed to create next.

They all sit there in a neat little row, waiting for me to do something, anything with them. Have I treated them right? If what Noland said is true, that these unique artisan brushes need to be treated with extra special care, then have I done them justice? Have they given me the motivation to paint with ease only for me to repay them with half-hearted rides in my back pocket?

Perhaps the reason why I feel so uncertain is that I haven't treated them the way I should. I've let them collect dry paint and dirt with nothing more than mild soap and warm water to barely wash them clean. The same way I've been told all my life to clean the useless store-bought brushes that can't compare. I suppose if I were treated the same as something so unimportant, I'd choose not to own up to my biggest talents, too. I can't blame these brushes. It's my fault for not remembering the lesson that was given specifically to care for them.

"I'm so sorry," my heavy heart tells the brushes. And I am.

I pick one up and give it a look over. The poor soft bristles are glued together with speckles of green paint. The handle has smudges of yellows and blues. I don't even remember the colors exactly. It's like the electric blue on my floor. Somewhere in my autopilot mode, the color must have gotten there, I just wasn't conscious enough to remember.

That's what happens when I drop into the creative zone. There's no breaking me out of it for anything, especially to inspect how much or how little the paint was spreading to the handles of my new brushes.

I dig out a towel from a set of plastic drawers where I keep ribbons and buttons and, well, towels, of course. As I pull the terrycloth out, I fold it in midair and place it next to the castor oil on the table. There. My cleaning station is all set up and I'm ready to try this out to clear my head and get back into the game of creation.

Unscrewing the lid to the caster oil, an earthy scent seeps into the open. It's like fresh dirt on a rainy day, only better. And it feels like comfort, a reminder of why I chose to pick up the paintbrush in the first place.

Then, I choose the speckled brush. The bristles are long and gather together, like a tiny ponytail of dark brown strands. They're soft and delicate, yet equally as strong. I feel both sickened and foolish, thinking of shampoo ads and conditioner commercials.

I flick the ponytail between my fingers, imagining a model putting her hair up at the end of the day. I run my fingers along its edges and imagine the hair model running her hand through hers. A mock-commercial voice-over plays in my head, talking about restoration and cleansing as if what I'm about to do is the same process as *Head and Shoulders* or *Suave*.

It's just fox hair, I remind myself. *It's just mink*, I'm convinced. *Or backyard squirrel*. Even though I'm not so sure backyard squirrels come in this specific shade of brown.

But that has to be exactly why they're so soft and spread so smoothly. They're a piece of functional art of their own, and will never fray or poke out in all directions. Not if I ensure I take care of them.

The person who made these must have thought of both their longevity and function. They must have thought about their hold and appearance. They must have put a little of themselves into each one, as artists tend to do with their best work.

A piece of themselves. My fingers run along the handle again, admiring its perfect imperfections. Little bumps and ridges and curves that feel both natural and purposeful. There's definitely a piece of the artist's story in here somewhere.

A deep inhale as I contemplate what story I have or what piece of myself is worth sharing in my own work. Could there be something I'm missing? Something I could explore more of myself? Something that would say why it is I have to give this last painting my all?

For myself?

For the Volga girls?

I've. Got. Nothing.

The green-speckled brush is in my hand again, and before I treat the bristles, I meticulously go over the handle, plucking off whatever specks of paint I can with my chipped fingernails. They fly off like discolored dandruff and already I feel a little better. Even though this wasn't a part of Noland's lesson, I have to believe it'll help. It's not like I can treat one piece of the brush like royalty and the rest like trash. That's like giving your face a wash, but leaving your armpits up to chance.

I hold the now clean handle and dip the bristles into the jar. They fan out, like hair in a swimming pool. I move it back and forth, watching each strand swim in the oil in soft movements. It's a trippy movie sequence in front of my eyes, only without a soundtrack. Wavy shapes and splashes of color dance and sway in a drunken rhythm. It's hypnotic. And it kind of makes me feel like I'm washing away my thoughts.

A few more moments pass. Or a thousand. I have no idea, but it's time to check in with myself again. In such a liquid state, I should be able to find something of myself to put on canvas.

Right?

Nope. Still nothing. Nothing that feels important enough. Nothing that feels like it's worth sharing with the world. I'm just a 20-year-old college dropout who's still trying to figure out why the heck she was put on this earth in the first place.

Frustrating.

Maybe I shouldn't think too hard, just let it happen and all that. Let this liquid state take over me and assume whatever is supposed to happen, will happen. That's how great art is created, right?

So, I quiet my thoughts and dip the brush back in. It's just me and this brush, and a puddle of oil at the bottom of a jar.

When I finally pull it out of the oil, I watch the thick droplets leave the bristles and find their way back into the jar, where they lose their individuality and wait for the next brush to disturb the collective.

It does. Again and again, my fingers and the brushes repeat this dance. And each time, it's more mind-numbingly satisfying to watch the little ponytails swim in the oil, and all the debris loosen and fall away.

Noland was right; this is cleansing. Not just for my tools, but for me, too.

We could all do with a good cleansing now and again.

The towel welcomes each brush in a neat row and I look at the glistening globs of bristles. They're shining, gorgeous. Better than any shampoo model has displayed on television. I touch the end of one of my braided pigtails and wish that my hair looked half as good as these paintbrushes do. I guess that's what I get for using the cheap dollar-store brand of shampoo on my own head: dry and brittle hair. When I pull away my fingers, a few blonde strands break off. Yet, when I touch any of these brushes, the strands are strong, sturdy. They look *healthy*. Making a mental note to do something about that later.

Find a way to cleanse myself a little more than my brushes.

As I work each bristle in the towel, wiping away the left behind oils, I pet the ends. They're so soft, and I can only imagine what it would be like to paint with them now. I wipe the last one clean and admire the row in front of me. I do feel a little more relaxed. I can't even figure out what time it is.

But I hear the bang of the basement door and feet racing down the steps. Whatever part of the day it is, it's Livvy time now.

"Emily Ellis!"

Uh oh, she's stressed.

"What's wrong, Livvy?"

Her eyes are wide and bloodshot, and her brown skin is glistening in sweat. Whatever is eating at her is making her real nervous. It's making the stress itself come out in her voice and show up in her eyes. The thing that catches my attention, though, is the oversized Joe's coffee mug in her hand.

She pants out a response, "I just came from Joe's."

152

"I see that." I point to her mug. "Looks like you were in such a hurry, you didn't bother putting away your dirty mug in the return bin."

"Shoot. I carried it all the way here." When she talks, her voice sounds distant, like her body is one place and her mind is in another. It's freaking me out so much that I can hear my heart pounding in my ears.

"Livvy?" I hope to call her back here, to my basement, but even though she is looking at the mug in her hand, her gaze is through it.

"Livvy?" I step toward her and the sound of my foot hitting the concrete floor startles her. Her body jolts, her face shoots at me, and her mug drops to the floor. It shatters into a pile of jagged pieces.

"Oh my gosh, I'm so sorry, Girl. I'll clean it up."

I throw my hands up and ask her to sit, right there on the stairs where she had paused her last step. Then, I walk over to the pieces and gently collect them in my hands. They're like crude pieces of Chihuly, before they're painted beautifully, before they are fused together, before they transform into art with a message.

"What's eating at you, Liv?" The last shard is triangular and sharp, and as I pick it up, I'm glad there aren't any dusty bits that will get lost in the floor cracks to be found later by someone's bare feet.

She shakes her head free of her daze. "Beans, Mills."

"Beans? Livvy, didn't we do this already?"

She bites her lips and nods, the curls on top of her head bouncing with the movement. "Beans," she whispers. "I read up on beans. Remember how I mentioned I was reading up on them?"

How could I forget? "So, like, green beans? Or coffee beans or?"

"More like fava, kidney, and," she takes a deep breath, "mung."

"Mung beans, right." It doesn't sound appealing, and it sounds less understandable. I want to catch up to her knowledge, but she's already a thousand steps ahead of me. "Liv, you're going to have to break it down for me."

153

"Fava beans have this glycoside called vicine in it. Which is toxic to some people."

"Toxic? As in poisonous?" That does sound like a problem. "Livvy, what do you mean by some people?"

"As in, if you have a hereditary loss of the enzyme glucose-6-phosphate."

"Livvy, you're talking Greek to me."

She inhales and slows down. "Basically, if you have a problem with the way your red blood cells break things down, then you can get sick from eating fava beans."

"Okay. Check on family history before I chow down on a bowl of fava beans. Noted."

"Good call, Mills." She doesn't miss a beat. "And kidney beans have this toxin called Phytohaemagglutinin that causes stomach bugs."

My ears tingle with the idea. "You mean something like food poisoning?" Could this be what killed Malory, Andrea, and Sam?

She nods enthusiastically. "Exactly like food poisoning. Stomach cramps, bathroom running, and all around really gross sickness all day and all night."

"But running to the bathroom doesn't cause death, right?"

I can feel the weight of both our hearts get heavier. "No. It doesn't."

We're back to square one. "What was the last bean you read about?"

"Mung bean. Sounds real cool, but they're just weird sprouty things people eat on their salad."

"Nothing toxic?" It really seemed like she was really onto something. She came here all hopeful and out of breath, and yet so quickly, it seems like we've both been let down by her epiphany.

"Not unless you leave them out too long and they grow bacteria. Then, you know, it's just like any other spoiled food."

"So, unless Malory, Andrea, and Sam all ate a sour bucket full of a fava and kidney bean mix, then I guess that's not what got to them, huh?"

"It's unlikely. But also, something happened to them, right? And if the theory is some kind of food poisoning, then maybe I'm onto something, right?" Her panicked gaze has grown hopeful, and I know her mind was working faster than her rationality could keep up.

"Maybe, Liv. Maybe." I want to believe that she's close. I want to believe that a couple of girls from small town Volga could piece together the mystery of the dead girls. I want to believe that we could stumble across some kind of knowledge that would clear things up.

So that we could be their voices for them.

So that my painting can come to life and be a microphone for their voices.

I pick up the jar of oil in front of me and tilt it back and forth. The colorful paint specks left behind float in the ooze to one side, and when I shift the way I'm holding it, they lazily float toward the other.

It looks like I need a completely different cleanse to clear out my head. I'm not so sure castor oil has done the trick. Not fast enough.

"Say, Livvy, when you need to clear your mind, what do you do?"

"Run," she says without skipping a breath. "I run."

I was afraid she'd say that.

"Think Stark will help transfer the paintings I've already finished to the gallery?"

She gives me a wink. "Without even asking, I guarantee it. It'll give you guys a little time to bond, too!"

I roll my eyes. "No time for bonding, Liv. I need him to take them there so I can run."

Her eyes grow into saucers. "Run?"

"If it works for you, I'm gonna see if it works for me, too."

CHAPTER TWENTY-ONE

Him

They've really done a lot to this place. It used to be a run-down little shop, empty for months on end. The only time it's ever filled and open is in October when a costume store moves in for a few weeks. And even then, it's draped in black plastic sheets and cheap purple lights. And every year, kids flock and tippy-toe to it and buy up the plasticy one-size-fits-all costumes, paint their faces in cakey face paint, and call themselves creative. It's a gaudy amateur's wet dream and my own personal nightmare.

But now? I look around this place and it looks nothing like the phantasm of creativity. It's brilliantly lit with spotlights in the center of each wall, illuminating brightly colored canvases and 3D paintings and all the colors and brush strokes that have been recruited specifically for this.

For us.

And soon, for me.

Under each hung art piece is a shiny plaque, meant for the title of the piece and the name of the recruit. And at the end of each line of recruit pieces is an empty space with an extra light shining on it. This is meant for a mastery, his or her creative genius that supports their recruit. Their last hurrah to say, "Me and my recruit, us together, we deserve to move forward. We deserve to be seen. I deserve a seat in The Circle and this recruit has talent enough to share our vision with the world. We can do this together."

It's the proof we're all aiming for.

And there are only five spots in The Circle open.

Well, ten. Five masters and five recruits. And even then, I'm sure it's the masters who get first dibs on new vessels and new lifetimes.

And there are at least a dozen walls that are already filling up with the recruits' artwork.

Not everything is here, though. Mine sure isn't. Not yet anyway.

I'm not too concerned. She'll pull through. She'll get them in. Come Hell or high water, she's going to push through and get done what needs to get done. After all, she wants those paintings to be seen.

Or heard.

Or something like that.

Until then, it's time to scope out what I'm up against. I'm standing in front of a display nearly full of existential canvases, my palms damp with nervous sweat. These are good. Real good. I know so not just with my eyes, but with my body, too. Simply being in their presence makes my skin tingle and my breaths shallow.

This isn't just art; it's movement. I have to stop my hand from reaching out and touching the brushstrokes because it's so damn good. I wish I could touch what this artist touched. I wish I could feel what they felt. I wish I could be inside this artist, feeling out where their talent lives, grab hold of it, and wrap it around my little finger to keep and call on whenever my heart needs it.

My hands find themselves and I consciously make my fingers interlock. No. I can't allow myself to dive that far into this. This is my competition. It has no place by my side when I so desperately need to assure what's under my thumb gets done to the best of its ability.

Not its… hers. Her ability.

I know she can do it. I've had the same reaction to her work before. Well, similar reactions. But there isn't an alternative. And even finding out if there is isn't an option. There's no time left, and this recruit is the only one who has crawled inside of me from day one.

No; she's the right one. And if she needs a little push, I'll give it to her. Whatever it takes to harness her talent to pass. There is no other option I can't not pass. Not passing means leaving. And leaving means accepting failure. Failure means death.

Like I said, it's not an option.

Clearly, the handler who brought in the recruit responsible for the display in front of me considered the same thing. I don't know who that handler is or how they found their recruit, but there's one very clear path ahead of me. I need to find whoever it is and rattle them up as much as possible. Make him falter. Fail. Sweat under his brow and fizzle. But when I go to the spot for his work at the end, it's empty. No work, no plaque, no identity at all.

Damn.

So I turn a corner and observe the next wall of art. This one isn't as impressive. In fact, it's so underwhelming I'm sure it won't even be in the running for The Circle. I don't even bother looking for a masterpiece there. It's not worth the effort. The wall next to it is completely blank, just like mine. It's an unknown competitor, but my brain has to tell me that it'll be just as underwhelming. I don't have enough space in there to add to my concerns.

A draft from the front door sneaks to my arms. Any minute, I'm sure someone will be in to fill in my wall. Oh, what it would be to watch the looks on the other handlers' faces when they see what I'm bringing in.

But the front door closes, and the only people who entered are carrying in cherub paintings that belong in some kitschy artisan shop somewhere. Not at a gallery as important as this.

Around another corner, I see another wall that's started to fill with a single painting. But this one? It doesn't just make my skin tingle. It puts my entire being on fire. Each stroke of paint is painfully expressive. I can hear the recruit's agony through their color choice and quick hits of splatter. And even though I'm not typically a fan of abstract creations, this one has crawled under my skin.

Better than the wall of paintings that made me tingle.

Scarily close to how *hers* have made me feel.

I can't let this one live in the hidy spots of my soul. This one doesn't deserve to live there. I need to let this one go, tear myself away, and I need to accept my own recruit for all of her beautiful talents as they are.

"Pretty amazing, isn't it?" a man next to me says. He's short with a greying burly beard and he has a slight accent I can't place. Definitely not a man from around here.

I nod and cross my arms. "It definitely has potential, that's for sure."

"I was actually hoping you'd tell me otherwise."

He turns to me and grimaces. I can tell he wants to jut his hand out and offer a shake, but that's not how we do things around here. We don't touch the people who might seal their own fates with poor recruiting skills. When we're around our own, we make sure to fight the instinctual pleasantries and practice restraint. It keeps our strength up as we separate the normal world from ourselves and ourselves from what the normal world expects.

"So, this one isn't yours?"

He shakes his head. "Not in the slightest. Mine is the one in the front; easily the most satisfying collection so far." He gestures to the first wall of art I came across, and my skin tingles again. "And besides this one in front of us, I'm willing to bet my entry is the first to be accepted."

My heart summersaults. So this is the guy. This is the guy I need to rattle.

"I see." I scratch at my chin. I don't want to give this guy any indication that the collection he brought in has made an impression.

So I lie to myself the best way that I can. I tell myself his recruit is a sham. Nothing more than a wanna-be artist whose best showcase of talent comes from paint by numbers.

It's nothing. That display has done nothing. I barely even noticed it, that's how insignificant it is.

I tell myself it's time to make him feel overlooked. Less than. Make him think I couldn't care less. "I guess I skipped over that one."

"Well, you should really go back and make sure you take it in." His voice has dropped a couple of notes. He is challenging me.

It's nothing. Absolutely nothing. Boring, even.

I take away any confrontation I might have been putting off by uncrossing my arms and dropping them to the side. "Sure, I suppose I should give it another look. Anything that doesn't make a great first impression might just be better the second time around, right?" I give him a wink. The same wink that seems to put everyone at ease. The same wink that makes my recruit turn into putty at my fingertips.

"If it hasn't made an impression on you yet, then you flat out didn't see it, friend." Guess my wink doesn't work on fat burly men with a superiority complex.

"You said it was in the front, right?" I point in the same direction he was pointing at before. "Like, right when you walk in? I'm sure I must have seen it. Can't miss the first thing you're greeted with, right?"

"Then, friend, you must be blind."

"I assure you, I have twenty-twenty vision, *friend.*"

"Maybe you ought to schedule for your yearly vision test, because I'm telling you, if you had a look at what my recruit could do, you wouldn't even question what might fill up the rest of the building."

The chuckle that comes from me takes me by surprise. "Is that why you're standing here, asking for some reassurance that this," I point to the painting in front of us, "isn't going to be worthy?"

Got him. His face is red. His brows are sweaty. He is faltering. And if I were to wager a guess, he's feeling a little fizzled out and dizzy.

"I don't need your reassurance, friend."

160

"And I don't need yours. My eyes work perfectly fine. I just don't see what you apparently see in that recruit of yours."

"And what about yours? I suppose the work you've brought in is just breathtaking, isn't it?"

I shake my head. "Now if I were to tell you that, it would ruin the surprise."

"And what surprise is that?"

"Oh, just that I've done everything to ensure my name gets on the list for The Circle. I have literally put in everything. Not just hard work and preparation, but I've put in my soul. Hell, I've put in the souls of several."

The clippings. Those paintbrushes. The talent in each *thing*.

"That's what's so great about this recruit of mine. She doesn't waste anyone's time with art that doesn't do anything. She ensures that every piece has a piece of her and a piece of the stories she tells through her craft. It moves you. It literally reaches in and grabs hold of your emotions, adjusting them this way and that until you're completely tied up in the despair and curiosity and love and ability and reality and beyond."

I take in a deep breath. I want to make sure he understands what I'm trying to tell him. "In all my years, I've never seen anything like it, and I guarantee you haven't either. No, *friend*, it doesn't matter how grand or talented you think your recruit is because all that matters is that mine is more than enough to get me where I belong. I don't even need to tell you to go have a look to see for yourself. That's how sure I am. I don't need your approval. I believe in her work enough myself to know it'll pass."

With every word that spills out, my hands dampen even more. I have to make sure my words are steady because he needs to believe that I believe them, too. And I do. But I'm not delusional. There's always a chance that I'm wrong, that I won't impress the Dignitary like I need to, and I'll be forced to leave and live a life of my own death.

"Oh really, friend, and what name would that be? What name should I expect to be next to mine on the list?"

I turn my back on him and walk away. I'm not giving this man another moment of face-to-face time with me. But also, I want to be sure he hears me loud and clear. I want him to know the name of the man who out beat him in the recruiting stage so he could remember it for the rest of his short eternity.

"Noland Elsinger."

CHAPTER TWENTY-TWO

"Thanks for helping, Stark." I open up the door under the washing machine and point down the stairs. "Everything is down there. Just be careful of the fourth step down. That one is a little uneven."

Even though I knew he'd agree to help pack up and unload my paintings, seeing him here has my heart full and my cheeks hot.

"Got it." He eases a smile out as he gazes down the staircase. "So this is where you keep all your masterpieces? In a dark lair under your kitchen floor?"

What is it about the Landons and their superhero lairs?

Heat deepens in my cheeks. "I wouldn't call them masterpieces, Stark. They're just paintings. Nothing special."

"I'll be the judge of that."

If only he could be the judge. There's no telling who is actually going to take in my canvases during this gallery to determine what kind of price tag it's worthy of. That is, if I can even fill in that last painting requirement.

We step downstairs, one uneven step at a time. When we get to the fourth step, we both shift our weight to keep from losing our balance on it. Each step down, I feel a little more nervous. I'm not exactly sure why. Stark's seen my most provocative painting already. Everything after that is mild in content.

Well, except that they're the representation of dead girls. That's not exactly easygoing. I guess I'm mostly concerned with what his reaction will be.

Will he understand my work for what I intend it to be? Will he feel the girls' voices by seeing my rendition of their last views? Will he appreciate who they are both in theory and possible reality? Will their stories grip him the way they've gripped me?

Everything is quiet except our footsteps until I lead him over to the little alcove. I'm a little surprised he hasn't mentioned the gas stove or how I've decorated with fold out tables and chairs. I mean, I'm doing my best *Best Housekeeping* impression over here. "Everything's in the alcove," I tell him. "Like I said, I really appreciate your help. I would carry them all myself, but you know, I need to make the most out of the time I have and figure out what I need to do for the last canvas. Plus, it's a heck of a lot easier to use your truck than to skate them all down Main Street."

But he's not looking at the alcove. He stops in front of my wall mural and scratches the back of his neck. I can almost hear his breath hitch as his eyes take in the image in front of him. "It's no problem, Mills," he says half-heartedly. But the way his voice is barely a whisper, I know his mind is a million miles away. "This is-" He stops, seemingly to think about how to fill out the rest of the sentence. "This is-" His hand moves from the back of his neck to tracing his jawline.

And before I find myself trailing the same line with my eyes, I fill out the rest of the sentence for myself. "- a map of Volga."

"Yeah." He nods. "A pretty amazing map. Mills, this is incredible." His breath is back. I can hear him suck it in and let it out as he admires — *he's freaking admiring* — my painting.

Again, I'm stuck between appreciating his judging eyes and fearful of what they might mean.

"It's just some paint on the wall, Stark. Nothing too amazing about that." But my heart does a backflipping happy dance at the compliment. "Anyway, like I said, all my canvases are over here. All except the last one I still need to paint."

He scratches at his sharpened jaw again. "And what's that one going to be?"

"Stark, if I knew, it would already be done."

"Can I make a suggestion?"

I swallow. Nod. With that jawline, he can make any suggestion and I'd be glad to hear it. Maybe it could be that profile I enjoy so much.

Ugh, Livvy would have a field day knowing that.

"You."

Gulp.

Alright, heart rate, don't beat yourself out of the ribcage.

I shake my head, but I can't find the words to actually respond to his suggestion. Why is everyone suggesting *me*? What is it that I have that needs to be put on canvas?

I turn away from him so he doesn't see my cheeks flush. I don't want to have to answer to his proposal of a self-portrait. Not when I don't even know if it's worth it.

He follows me closer to the alcove, but I swear I can feel his attention drift toward that wall, analyzing my brush strokes and color choices, and the way each building and street is a unique shape, making it not so obvious that it's a map at all. Yet, he got it. It didn't take any kind of extra explanation or walkthroughs. I guess that's how it goes for someone who spends the majority of his time supplying tools and products to both the geniuses and the hacks in small town Volga.

It's like wine tasting, only for the visual pallet. He's refined his taste and knows what he likes.

He likes my work.

That thought trips up my mind and my feet, and I land myself in the corner of my supply table. "Ouch!"

"Are you okay?" He rushes forward and rests a hand on my shoulder. I can feel his warmth radiate through me.

Yup, I'm okay now.

"Yeah. Just a little clumsy is all." I give him a wide smile and turn back to the alcove.

I pull out two canvases, the dark starry one and the pearlish earring girl. They're both dark, gritty. I can feel myself fall back into their stories again. I'm almost in both places at both of the times and my heart breaks into pieces all over again. Before I allow it to show, I hand them over to Stark.

He takes them with ease and holds them up to the dim basement light. "Mills, these are incredible." And within a split second, I can feel him falling into the same place I've fallen into. I welcome it and fear it and am excited for it all at the same time.

Somewhere in the unspoken, he lands. Together, we float in the voices of the dead girls, feeling their stories and wondering how true they are. He looks at me. "I have no doubt you're going to get the attention you deserve."

"It's not about my attention, though. Not anymore."

He nods. "It's about those girls. Somehow, you've found a way to tell their stories."

I'm not sure how he knows. Maybe it's his artistic knowledge showing. Livvy always talked about how Stark used to doodle and draw. Apparently, he was really good. Maybe he's calling back a little bit of what he used to know. Or maybe he's getting it all from the paintings themselves. And if that's true, then I really have done my job well.

Good job, Mills.

All I can do is nod when he gazes back at me. My voice has disappeared and so has his. We're just two people floating somewhere between here and reality, where color theory and brushstrokes are the only words we speak. We're stuck in this ether together, like stretched canvas on a wooden frame, not really waiting for anyone to pick us up. We're just existing as we are.

His Adam's apple bobs up and down when he swallows back … his words? Nerves? I swallow, too. Mine is definitely nerves.

166

"Heyyyy, is the party all downstairs?" Livvy's voice rings from above, bringing the two of us back to reality.

"Um, yeah." I'm not sure if I've been staring at Stark for a minute, twelve, or an entire hour, but I still don't break my gaze as Livvy's steps sound through the basement.

"So, how are we doing this? Just pack up the truck and drive to the artsy place?"

Livvy's steps stop, and I blink over to her, now standing a few feet away. And how the heck did I end up only inches from Stark? I don't remember moving this close to him. It didn't seem like we were nearly touching just seconds ago. I didn't intentionally close the distance between us. But now with Livvy in my peripheral, I'm suddenly aware, very aware, of how close we actually are.

"Sorry. Am I interrupting something?" Livvy smirks. I can actually hear her crack a smile in her words.

Oh boy. I'm never going to hear the end of it from her.

"Not at all." I break out of my stance, quickly turn back to the alcove, grab the Crane painting, and hand it to her.

"You're just in time to help load up."

"And I get this one, huh?" She holds up the canvas. "Goody."

Laughing, I fold my arms over myself. "I figure it's a good story to tell. And besides, thanks to the dining hall leftovers that leaked out of the trash, you can't even tell who it was supposed to be anymore. It's not Crane. It's just some creepy guy."

"Yeah; the part of a horrible man hasn't gone away. I can still feel my nervous system tense up looking at it. And, look, if you squint, you can almost make out a face with long hair."

I squint and sure enough, it does look like a nondescript face with long hair. It's the perfect representation of the looming entity that takes away innocence. It doesn't have to have an exact identity. The fact that it's an eerie figure is enough.

167

I take the last painting from its spot and push past Livvy and Stark. I can hear an audible slap, and I bet it's Livvy smacking Stark's arm. He lets out a tiny, "Hey!" that I ignore because that's a brother and sister thing and I'm not going to put myself in the middle of that.

I'm well aware I'm *directly* in the middle of it. I'm just trying to step out of that middle and skirt on the outside, thank you very much.

We move like this all the way up the stairs. Me leading the pack, trying to ignore whatever silent banter is going on behind me about me, and Livvy and Stark shoving each other back and forth while holding onto their assigned paintings.

When we finally make it to the top of the stairs, we lay each canvas down on the kitchen table. One after another, it tells a story. From the result of rumors to the last sight of Sam Aleah. They tell a dual plotline that doesn't have an ending. On one hand, it's about the gone girls of Volga County. On the other, it's the message of listening. It says to quiet your own assumptions and open up to hearing and understanding the reality around you, even when it's difficult to listen to.

"Paint By Murders," I say.

"What's that?" Livvy says.

"It's the name of the collection."

"It's perfect," Stark says.

Livvy shoves him again. "It is," she agrees.

"I wouldn't mind owning an Emily Ellis original like this myself, someday."

I clench my jaw, swallowing down the heat wanting to yet again escape to my cheeks. "Well, you might have to wait on that, Stark. If I'm going to make it in time before the gallery opening, I'm going to use these for submission."

"I'm willing to wait, Mills," Stark says. And after an awkward silence, he asks, "So now what?"

"Now I figure out what the heck I do for my last painting. Liv, what is it you said you did to clear your head?"

She cocks her head to the side. "I run."

"Exactly," I tell her. "If I can't come up with anything tonight, I'll be going on a run tomorrow. I'll clear my head, and for sure be ready to show off what I can at the gallery auction."

"Emily Ellis, a runner?" Livvy's skepticism is thick in the air.

"Eh, how different could it be from skateboarding?"

CHAPTER TWENTY-THREE

There's something about the way Stark said it - wanting to own an Emily Ellis original - that made everything in my body jump into motion. It's like static electricity hit my heart and jolted currents into all my insides.

I know he didn't mean it this way, but that's a lot of pressure. And now I have to figure out how to put me - Emily Ellis - in a painting. For my sake, not someone else. Not the dead girls.

Ugh, it's so hard!

I spent all afternoon and night staring at a blank canvas, trying to picture myself in it. I tried to figure out exactly how I'm supposed to dive into my story. *My* story without taking away from someone else's. And yet, every time I tried to dip my brush into a pallet of paint, something stopped me. I couldn't figure it out. Nothing felt right. Nothing seemed right.

I ended up with… a blank canvas. Well, a blank canvas and this jittery feeling I can't shake. No can do.

I can't fight off those electric currents, so I do the only thing I can think to do. As uncharacteristic and crazy as it sounds, I run.

Thanks, Livvy, for that suggestion.

Now, I'm darting through traffic like a blonde headed version of Frogger. Each pigtail bounces on my back, making me wish for once I would have cut my morning routine in half and given myself a ponytail instead. My legs feel like liquid fire encased in skin-sacs, but I push through anyway, past the burn, past the hurt, and straight onto the place where I feel like I can do anything because my body can take it.

It's weird running instead of being on my skateboard. It feels slower and faster at the same time. But I felt like I needed to try something entirely new to break out of the funk I'm in and break into something that will kickstart the creativity of that last piece.

It was dumb of me to wear jeans. I shoulda grabbed a pair of sweats. Oh well.

I'm running back from the neighborhood that's right past campus. Joe's is nearby and I smell fresh coffee. Part of me wants to stop inside and grab a cup, but there is no time. If I don't get this piece done today, then my art career is done for. That, and whatever message I have already created with my other paintings will be erased into nothingness. The chatter of the crowded people inside tells me that Sam is an idea of the past and today's thoughts are only with hot oversized mugs of delicious bean water. I can't let Sam and the other girls get erased completely.

But then Stark's, "You," rings in my ears again. Painting me. Me. Me?

How the hell am I supposed to put *me* into a painting when all I can think about is the stories of the girls I've already painted?

My own story is being told. Right now. I still have a voice for myself. I don't need to paint it out on canvas hoping others will understand, do I? Stark seems to think so, but why?

Noland had a similar thought, too.

What do Noland and Stark see that I don't? What would a painting of *me* look like anyway? Because right now, all I can think of is that it might come out looking like a sad stick figure floating into nothingness. There's nothing to grab hold of, nothing substantial that would make people *feel* anything when they look at it.

That's not art. That's just sad.

My legs push faster, and I swear the muscles inside them are melting, they hurt so much. My stick-figure self is melting away with every forced step. But I'd rather melt away than the girls in my painting, so I push on, making sure my pace quickens.

171

I smell the same moldy trash that lives between Broad and Cumberland. A Spanish speaking lady is screaming, and her pots and pans are still banging. She doesn't think about the girl who was found right outside her window. She's only thinking about who's in her way of making dinner.

Faster and faster, I make my muscles work even harder. The dead girls' stories are alive within me, so I need to make my muscles remember them, keep them alive.

My little melted clock home is only two blocks away, so I speed up even more. I push even faster, and I ignore the way everything inside of me is screaming to stop. They want to seize up, then crumble from under me. I don't care, you stupid muscles. Stop complaining! I'll never stop! Not as long as these girls need their names remembered and their voices heard. I'll keep going on and on. I'll feel their pain because they can't anymore!

But my muscles don't stop complaining. They get louder. They're past the point of asking for forgiveness, and they give up like two jello molds attached to my hips. I can't feel anything past my waist, which makes it pretty difficult to stay up on two feet.

One more step, and I fall. Hard. I catch myself with my hands, but holy cow it hurts like the Dickens. Gravel is embedded in my palms, and even though I try to brush it off, there are still a couple of specks that have decided my flesh is now their home. Ain't that awesome.

"Shit," I curse at myself. I can't believe I allowed that to happen.

"Shit, shit shit." My exhaustion has taken over and I'm terrified to face what that means about Sam. And Andrea. And Malory. And anyone else who might be drifting away from the memory of Volga.

I sit back and let my legs recover. Or at least, as close to recovery as they can get. They're at least getting their feeling back, and it is painful. It's like when they fall asleep and get woken up by another person kicking them.

I have Livvy to thank for that simile.

But I don't have time to think about what that feeling means or if I'll be able to stand on them again. A hooded figure runs past me, and while the brief bit of wind it brings feels great against my skin, I get the feeling that whoever is running, is running away from something. The weird thing is, this hooded figure isn't wearing Alpha pink or Beta green. He or she isn't even in Zeta blue. The hooded figure is in grey. Just plain old grey. A regular sweatshirt that has nothing to do with the Greek sisters or brothers in Volga.

I force myself up on unsteady feet and tell my body to balance. I'm in luck because right in front of me is my house. I can see its foundation melting away into the pavement. But that's not where the running person came from. She or he came from Arch Road. Or, at least, I think they came from Arch.

I'm strong, at least stronger than before. I can go check it out.

So I do.

I force my legs to bring me to Arch Road, which is off to the side, almost an alleyway of its own. My right leg screams at my left and my left leg yells at my right. Neither of them are happy that I'm making them move, forcing them to solidify past their jello stage. No cars come and go this way, and even in the daylight, the sun doesn't light up this corner of the world enough for it to matter much.

I know there are two large trash bins this way because my front door faces it. Every time I leave my dilapidated house, I'm greeted by these two green trash bins as if they are the most friendly neighbors in the entire block.

Only, they're trash. And dark. And not very welcoming at all.

And right now, they're even less welcoming because they're not alone. Right between the two of them are two arms, splayed out like noodles, two legs, starfished out, and a face covered by a dirty cloth that's still halfway attached to the dumpster.

173

There's a body.
Another dead girl in Volga.

CHAPTER TWENTY-FOUR

My bile mixes with piles of trash nearby, and the smell is heavily acidic. It's a mixture I've never quite taken in before, and my body doesn't know what to do with it all.

My legs don't want to move, but my brain is screaming at me to stand up, run after the mystery man, or mystery woman, and tackle him — her — to the ground. I don't even remember falling to my knees, but here I am mentally screaming at myself to get up.

Brush it off, Mills. Get up. Just. Get. Up.

I want to stop this once and for all. I want to put an end to the dead girls in alleys, and splatter whoever has been doing this all over Volga county in the greatest piece of art I have ever created. I want to make a splash with his blood over the streets in the same way that these girls have thrown up all over them.

No more guessing. This has got to be a man's work. A selfish, cowardly man.

But the art I want to do? I want it to be bigger. And more graphic. I don't want anyone to think it was some form of accident, either, not like they've been fooled into thinking with these girls.

I want his blood all over the streets so he can never do this again. If it's five, then five is five too many. He should have to pay. At least five times over.

My last painting has nothing to do with me because none of this has anything to do with me. This isn't my story to have. It's theirs and it ends with his. The last page I paint needs to end with his name scratched out of existence.

I push myself up and stand on my jello legs. Sort of. They're so wobbly, they barely provide any foundation to stand on. But I need to go after him. I need to catch him. I need to make sure these girls' voices are heard through a message of rage and deliverance.

One step forward, and I fall again.

"Arghhhh!" my voice echoes throughout the block. I can almost see my house's siding slide off at the vibrations. Mental curses run through me. I shouldn't have pushed my muscles so hard. They're definitely not used to it, and now I'm paying for it.

I stand again, another two steps, and I fall. "Come back!" I yell, and get up again. My legs don't want to move. And the hooded man is gone. I don't know where he went, and by now he is long gone. Got away. This is not fair. This is not okay. This is not how this story ends. It can't be!

"Get back here!" I yell out to nobody.

All the cars on the main road are still going at their stupid slow pace, not paying attention to anything in my direction. I mean, why would they? There aren't any kitschy shops or bakeries over here. Just broken down houses, trash, and dead bodies. Nothing to see here, folks.

"COME BACK!"

I will the hooded person back to me. But my will isn't strong enough, and my voice isn't loud enough and they are too far away. Whatever will I have left is breaking under the pressure. Both the pressure I put myself under and the pressure this mystery man has forced on me.

I double over. "Come back," I almost whisper, and my chin puckers up, knowing how futile it is and mad I can't force my body after the one person who knows anything about this.

"Ms. Ellis, is that you?"

I wipe my burning eyes. That voice. That familiar voice that has always been a call for calmness, a soothing sound to break me out of any trance. I don't know how he found me or what put him here, but thank goodness. Noland is here. His kind eyes are wide with fright as he looks down to the girl on the street and then to me.

"Oh, Mills, come. Let's get you out of here."

I shake my head vigorously. "No. I can't. I-" I jab my finger to the girl on the ground while averting my eyes. I can't look at her. I can already see Malory and Andrea and Sam in her. "She...she…" I can't find the words to describe what is in front of me and how it's affecting me, how it should be affecting him and everyone else around me. And why in the world is no one else stopping? Why isn't anyone doing anything? How can this not crumble the entire world around me because it feels like it's tearing everything inside of me to pieces?

Noland's strong arms wrap around me. I can feel their warmth soak into my skin, easing my shaking body and comforting the complaints of my muscles. It feels good. Safe. And I am so glad he is here. He gets it. He gets me. And he's taking away every bit of awfulness that has gotten into my veins and swam inside of them.

"Come. I've already made a call. There's nothing else we can do here. Come; let's get you home."

I return the squeeze he gives me, and even though a piece of me knows I shouldn't leave whoever this girl is here, alone, and without anyone to care about who she is, there's a bigger piece of me that wants to walk away from this. I want to recover my muscles and make a plan to gather my strength and face the man who did this. I will absolutely need strength to take care of him the way he took care of others.

Gone.

Noland smells amazing. A ton better than the scent I just covered myself with. It's like a mixture of honey and cedar, a welcoming scent after being hit in the face with death and puke. My hair under his nose probably smells horrible, but he doesn't let on that he notices. He just holds me tight to make me feel secure and safe. I hope I can draw from his strength to build up mine.

We stay like that for a moment before he repeats himself, "Come on. Let's get you home." I don't fight off his help as he wraps one arm around me and guides my legs across the street. Our feet move together like an awkward three-legged race, only he is doing most of the work. I am so thankful for that. I'm so tired. My muscles are tired and my head is tired and I am ready to sit down in a quiet room with Noland there to hold me up.

It seems like it takes hours to cross the tiny road and reach my doorstep. When we are finally there, Noland helps himself to the front door and lets us both in. He adjusts a chair at the sad little table that was left for me and sits me down in it. I look up at him and I know I must look like a sad, messy little girl sitting under a sad, melting clock. But he has protected me this far so I'm okay being vulnerable in his presence.

"You said you called?" My words feel foreign in my throat. I still haven't processed what, no sorry, *who*, I have come across.

"Called?" he parrots back as if the words sound foreign to him, too.

"Yeah. You said you called the police, right? They're coming for her, right?"

He nods silently, but doesn't say a word.

"Maybe we should have stayed there, Noland, you know? Maybe we should have seen if we could help her? Won't we get into trouble for leaving her?"

His head shakes now. "No. There was no helping her, Mills. You saw her. She was beyond help." He puts a hand on the top of my head and pushes my stray hair back behind my ear. One day, I'll be able to keep it in my braids. "But you're okay now. You don't have to worry about a thing."

I nod. Okay. Sure. That makes sense. I am okay. I'm here. I'm in my house. Safe. Sound. My heart is still beating. It wants to be the heck out of my chest and jump onto the floor, but it's still beating. So I must be okay, right?

But the girl across the street is not okay.

And that makes bile rise in my throat again. Before I have any time to react, it's out in the open and spread across my floor in a puddle of not a whole lot. I surprise myself. I thought I had already spilled everything my stomach had to offer across the street. And yet, here's a little gift for myself. More sick to swim in. Thanks, Self. You just keep on giving.

Noland pulls my hair back. He strokes it like a pet, and honestly, it feels good. I want him to keep doing it. I want him to keep petting me like a good girl so I can feel something that isn't so awful and emptying.

"You know what I do to feel better when I get upset?"

I wipe my mouth with my sleeve. A sticky strand of mucus trails like slug juice on the fabric. I would feel ashamed, except Noland never looks at me in a way that says I should feel embarrassed about anything. I'm comfortable here. I feel like I can drop any of the walls I might have built up with snark and humor, not that this is the time for that anyway, so I look at him dead in the eyes and wait for merciful advice.

What could possibly make me feel better? I really hope he doesn't tell me to clean again. I can't do that right now. I don't exactly feel like pulling out brushes and oils and solvents or whatever.

"I paint." He smiles at me, and I realize he is brilliant.

Painting. Yes. That makes sense. Painting might be exactly what I need to do. It might be the exact thing to take me from a sad puddle of vomit and tears to something useful. Noland is right. I do have a talent and I can use it.

Every time I have felt anything close to an empty feeling, I've immediately felt a spark after. Every time I've stepped into the shoes of these girls, I would picture what they might have seen. I'd grab my materials and let the piece speak through my hands without my brain even understanding what they're doing.

I think about my murder board downstairs and how all those little dotted circles have added up to not much, but now, with this girl…

"Would you like to paint, Mills?"

I nod. I would like to paint. Painting would give me some normalcy. It'd bring me back to reality and a path to process everything. It would give my body and mind both something to do other than internally scream through my external numbness.

But I need help getting down the steps. I could probably stand up okay, but my muscles are still asking for help. My heart needs the help, too. There is no way I'm going to be able to walk down those stairs without breaking my own neck and becoming the next of the dead girls in Volga.

Noland walks across the kitchen and lifts the door on the floor. It creeks its welcome, and I want nothing more than to race down there and process the emotions swimming inside of me. Make sense of what's happened and continues to happen. Maybe if I try hard enough I can even figure out who that strange man was who ran from that alleyway. I'm curious which colors will speak to me this time. Which ones will help my new art piece reveal itself? What's the story that's hiding within them?

Noland holds me up, and I can feel how strong he is. I can lean into him and feel like I'm more secure than if I had full control over my legs by myself. We get to the fourth step and he helps me lean toward the left to keep us from wobbling. He must have some kind of instinct for that. When we reach the bottom, he faces us at the mural map. My murder mural.

He pushes his long hair behind his ear. "Your talent, Mills, is amazing. I have honestly never seen anything like it. Not even the most seasoned artists can compare to what your hands are able to do." He holds my shoulders and turns around to look me in the eyes. "You put so much of yourself into them, it's quite literally breathtaking." He looks behind him, at a now empty table with leftover paints and my special brushes he gave me. "Come. You should paint."

He pulls over a folding chair and sits it at the table. I can feel his hands guide me to it and my body obeys. As I sit at the table in a stiff chair, I see a canvas appear in front of me. Somehow, Noland has already prepared a pallet, too. Blobs of the primary colors make a dotted triangle, and smaller blobs of black and white sit in the middle of them.

Anything is possible with a blank canvas and these few colors. Anything could form in front of me. Anything at all. I reach my hand up to the table, expecting a brush to be waiting for me, but there is none there.

"Ah, I'm so sorry, Mills. Let me help you."

"I can do it." I'm still in a daze, unsure of who I walked away from and what I'm supposed to be doing, but I reach for one of my special brushes.

"No, no, Mills. Here. I have something better for you."

And he hands me a new brush. One I hadn't seen before. The handle is similar. It's another knotted piece of polished wood. But the bristles are entirely different. These bristles have bunched up, curled texture to them. It's almost as if they move on their own, bending and twisting as if they are alive and reaching out for something to grasp a hold on. They're a sculpture of their own, a beautiful piece of artwork I haven't yet seen in brush form.

"It's brand new, Mills. No one has ever painted with it. Now, you can. This belongs to you."

So I do. I'm curious to test it out, with its bristles sticking out in different directions. And while it doesn't hold water like my other brushes do, it makes creating textures fun and sporadic. It really does have a life of its own.

My hand sweeps this way and that. I have no control over the colors I'm choosing nor do I have any idea of what's being formed. The paintbrush is in charge, telling me which direction to go, and I listen. I'm the medium, and the brush is calling a spirit.

I don't even realize how true that is until I make the final stroke and look down. There are no strong outlines, the entire painting is texturized in a way that gives an impression of what it is. This is it. This is my final art piece that's going into my portion of the gallery.

And it's the girl by the trash cans.

It has no likeness to classical art. I'm not calling in Picasso or Rembrant on this one. That's because none of those studied pieces of art can compare to the face I see in front of me. The face I know so well. The face that has been behind me forever and a day and has supported me even when I've made stupid decisions that I shouldn't.

A tsunami wave hits me. It's Livvy. The girl on the street was Livvy. She *is* Livvy. And all I did was stand there. This was my best friend through thick and thin and I just left her there to sit, to lay, to wait for who? Not for me. Not for the coward who wouldn't even go after the mystery man running from her body.

Her body. How the hell was that her body? She was fine the last time I saw her.

Her body. How could Livvy go quickly from being Livvy to being Livvy's *body*?

That's when I realize, the last time I saw her was literally the last time I'll see her again.

"Livvy!" My voice barely creeps out. What does go out into the open is painful. It's broken glass in my throat to say her name.

A heavy tear runs through my heart as it breaks into sand-like pieces. And heat rises with it when I feel anger bleeding through me. How could I have left her like that? When she was the lioness always looking out for me, ensuring my interests were first in our friendship. She kept me on my toes and fought for the truth as much as she could for me.

She was my pillar of strength, and I left her there to crumble.

The thought makes me hate myself, and I buckle in two. I don't even care that my muscles are still sore. The pain I'm feeling is so trivial compared to whatever it was that she went through. And all I can picture is the hooded man running away.

My fist bangs on the table and I stand up. I don't care if my legs end up breaking in half, I'm going after him.

"Whoa, whoa, whoa. Hold on there, now." Noland eases his hand on my shoulder and I can feel a little bit of the anger drip away. "You're in no shape to get all agitated. Look at what you created. Look at what you did." He holds up the still-wet picture.

The paint glistens under the overhead light, and I can see where the last brush strokes landed.

"Do you see what you did? You put your heart into this piece so fully that the feeling is running through you right now. Amazing, Mills. Amazing."

But I shake my head. It's not amazing. It's heartbreaking. And if Livvy were here, she'd tell me that what would make it good art is me feeling good about it.

I don't feel good. I feel broken.

"I don't know what it is, Mills, but you have always been above the other students. You were born with a piece of talent I haven't seen in anyone else in a long time. And no matter what I try, I, myself, have never been able to match that."

Even though I don't want to sit anymore, he guides me back down to my seat. Before I can realize what's happening, he hands me the brush I just painted with and the jar of castor oil.

"Go ahead. Clean it," he says.

Nothing else makes sense to me at the moment, so I do. I dip it in and I watch the curly bristles wave around in the oil a little. The last of the paint glides off and pools in the jar in a little collection of the only shade of orange you can use to associate a lioness with. The bristles don't soak it up as well as the other brushes, but the oil coats them in a sheen that makes them look healthy, alive.

Something about these bristles makes me miss Livvy more. They remind me of the way she used to pull her hair up on the top of her head. I'd admire the curly puffs that would sit on top as if they were specifically placed up there on a perch to watch the rest of the world happen around them.

"Is it clean?" Noland asks.

I lift it up to show him. A drip of oil runs down the stick-like handle and coats my fingers.

"Good girl," he tells me as he takes it from my hand and uses a towel to clean off the excess.

"Now, are you going to continue to be a good girl?"

I don't really know how to answer it, but the only answer that I can summon up is to nod, so that's what I do. Sure, I'll be good. I'll paint a picture. I'll jump up and race my legs to track down the mystery man wherever he went, even if it is across town. Or country. Or around the world. I'll do whatever it would take to bring my friend back. But if being good means to sit here for now, then I'll sit down and wait.

"Good. Then I need you to listen to me." Noland reaches across the table to grab a pair of scissors I must have left out without properly putting away. Then, he reaches into his back pocket and pulls out a comb.

I knit my brows. My first thought is maybe he has a nervous tic I had never noticed before, like combing out the hair in his face. But he doesn't touch his hair. He touches mine. He leans over and grabs hold of a pigtail. His hand gently wraps around the bottom and slides off the hair tie keeping it in place. His fingers rake through my braid to loosen it up, and he smiles when his work is almost done.

The comb feels nice on my scalp. It's like a massage that wakes up every blood cell under my hair, and my body wants to lean into it. My eyes close while I focus on just this feeling because I know if I don't, I'll start thinking about how Livvy never could brush out her hair without it being wet. The texture never would allow her. Wide toothed combs and detangling brushes were reserved for wash days.

And now I am thinking of that, and the more I try not to think about it, the more I do. I can't stop picturing her face, her laughter, and the way she would break out into some weird fact about beans.

Beans. What did she say about beans? Some of them had poison, right? Something that made people sick?

My eyes begin to burn, but before I can release anything from them, I hear a *snip* from behind me. The sound stops all trains of thought.

"What was that?" My voice is shaky, unsure of what just happened and what I should expect. Surely Noland didn't just cut my hair... did he?

He doesn't answer, but I see his pinched fingers slide their way into my vision. A little bundle of blonde hair is dangling between his thumb and forefinger, and the sight stops my heart from making a full beat.

"What did you do?" Which isn't exactly the question I want to ask. I want to ask, "What the Hell, Noland!?" and "What's your deal?" and "What are you going to do with *that*?" because it is just hair. But seeing it in his grasp like that, I know it's not just hair right now. He has a reason for this, I'm sure. I'm just terrified to find out what that reason is.

Without a word, he pulls out a stick — a *stick* — from his pocket. If I wasn't confused enough before, I sure am flummoxed now. What is he going to do with a damn stick?

Another reach into his pocket and Noland pulls out a piece of string. Here this man is, with a Mary Poppins pocket from hell pulling out everything under the sun to make my skin crawl. When he places it next to the stick and I see all the pieces together, the puzzle gets put together.

185

Noland is making a paintbrush. One of his special paintbrushes. And he's making it with my hair.

I pick up the brush I just used to make the lioness painting and touch the bristles that aren't bristles. There's a reason why this texture felt so familiar.

Livvy.

My hand is shaking so much that I can't hold on to the brush any longer. It drops and rolls onto the floor. I jump up from my seat as fast as I can and try to think about what I'm supposed to do next. What would make me a good girl? What would make me a good artist? What would make me a good friend?

My legs don't want to work after resting so long. The muscles feel locked into place, but I encourage them to move, no matter how stiff they want to be. So I move at a pace that's crawlingly painful over to my mural.

Halfway there and Noland calls after me, "You really need to take care of your things better, Emily Ellis."

My full name grates against my ears, but I keep moving. I don't care that he's picked up my Livvy brush from the floor, and I don't care that he's adjusting the hair with his scissors to ensure that it still could pass as bristles to anyone who might get their hands on it.

All I care about is the little bit of black paint left on the pallet he gave me. I dip my finger in it and lift it to the mural map in front of me.

I place my finger on the cinder block and draw a circle where I saw Livvy, right across the street.

That's when I realize it. That's when I see the pattern.

All the dead girls from Malory to Livvy have made a straight line that leads right to my house.

It all leads here, where I'm standing. When I turn around to face Noland, he gives me a smile. He's finishing up on wrapping the string around my hair and the stick to attach the two.

The memory of signing paperwork to this house hits me like a brick.

The Elsinger who owns the place, the Elsinger who hired the rental company to middle man the paperwork, the Elsinger who patched up what he could and left the rest… is the same Elsinger who took careful steps into my house, including the fourth step down to the hidden basement.

Noland Elsigner owns this house. And Noland Elsinger killed those girls.

CHAPTER TWENTY-FIVE

Noland

Poor Emily Ellis. She's figured it out. Well, she's figured some of it out, anyway. At least the part she's painted on the wall. And the part she painted on canvas.

What she hasn't figured out is that each of those girls was potentially in her position. They could have easily been a recruit if they had harnessed their talents in the way she has. But they never did. They showed the world a taste of what they could do and dangled that taste in the air never to be touched on again. Such a shame, really.

She also hasn't figured out why she's been chosen. She hasn't seen what her future holds. She doesn't get that I have watched her growth since before the first day she stepped foot on Volga's campus. And she definitely doesn't understand that because of me, that growth has doubled, tripled, to become the potential she is today.

Because of me, she has a future. A real future, where her soul will live on forever as it's meant to be.

But all that will come later. For now, I'll appreciate the conclusions she has come to. Brilliant, really. I highly doubt anyone else in her position would have come to the same conclusion, to paint a map of this town and draw a line straight to where I led her. Right here, in her house.

Well, my house.

Well, not even that. Not anymore. Not that I need a place to call my own. I'll have a more permanent place once I'm in The Circle. Which will happen. It has to happen. There's just one more step to securing it.

True, recruits need four paintings. But like recruit, like handler: I have yet to finish my own piece to go with hers. Now that she's finished her final piece, I need to finish mine. The entire collection will solidify our spots — my spot, with her talent by my side.

How I need that talent. Every inch of it. I wish I could absorb it with every fiber of my being instead of just holding it. Not that I haven't tried before. I have. But that was... different. It wasn't right. None of them had the talent that I could use or take or share or explore.

I just used what I could and then trashed the rest.

Speaking of, I make my way over to the little gas stove, the one that has treated me so well for so long. It's been there through the thick and thin, making all the oil I need for myself and for her. It's the reason I have a stash of powder. A stash of sleep dust. A stash of trash-be-gone.

I light the stove and grab my materials from the little cabinet sitting next to it. A handful of caster beans drop into a metal pan, all ready to boil up and turn into gold.

I won't need my powder for her, not now. Hopefully not ever. But I will need her to understand how special she is. How much she is needed. All the others were so disposable. It's hard to believe I ever thought otherwise. They were mediocre tools at best.

But this one, this Emily. This Mills. She's the key to it all. And if I could take her talent and absorb it like a sponge, then we'll both end up where we're supposed to be. Me, in The Circle, and her providing her purpose. My purpose. Ours.

This is so grand.

I pinch the ends of her hair together, the little clump of fantastic, and wrap the string around one more time. Ah, it's so perfect. With every brush I create, each one gains a little more personality and a little more perfection.

This one, though? This soft blonde tuft? It has more potential in it than all the others combined. Especially that last one. I'm shocked that she was able to do anything with it. Not only was that texture completely wrong for my use, but the source it came from was not up to par.

There was no artistic talent in her. She just got in the way. And when she approached me with all this scientific nonsense about how I'm poisoning people with beans, I knew I had to eliminate her. Beans. Laughable. As if I could poison anyone with beans. It's not my doing at all. It's theirs. If they can't handle my special drink, then that's on them. That includes her. Goodbye, useless sidekick. She's mine now.

Tacking the string down is always a little tricky. I take a small ball of hard wax from my pocket and press it on. In my other pocket is a lighter. Always handy for when the creative bug bites, especially when that bug is caged up and sassy enough to strike at any time.

"I've been thinking about it, Mills."

She jolts at my voice. Good. She hears me. She's broken the trance she was in. This is the first time I'm going to let her in on a piece of the truth, and I need her attention.

I dab the drying wax with the pad of my thumb. Everything is tight, sound. It's ready to go.

"In order to paint like you, I need a piece of you."

Why do her eyes widen? Doesn't that make sense? In order to have art — *good* art — you need to put a piece of the artist in it. Doesn't she know this? Didn't I teach her?

She makes good art. Scratch that, she makes art perfection. There's no way I could do what she does unless there's a piece of her in it, too. There was proof of that when I tried out all the other handmade brushes for myself.

It was all crap. Nothing good enough for consideration of The Circle. It has to be her.

Holding up my newly crafted brush, I examine it. Little blonde hairs droop over like a ponytail. I'm sure her cute braided pigtails will never look exactly the same again. One might be a tad shorter than the other. But that's the sacrifice she needs to make for the good of the world, for my part in The Circle.

But that tiny ponytail? It's not perfectly perfect. That's just going to flaccidly droop into paint and splatter it around like a fish. That won't do. It needs to be taught, pointed, and ready for action.

I shake my head and pull out a tiny pair of scissors from my pocket. That's the great thing about men's jeans, you know. We can have our own deep cave right on our hips to fill with anything we want to. A teensy snip here, a tiny snip there, and the ends shape up into a delectable shape perfect for crafting.

Now it's ready.

Now, she'll be ready.

I make my way over to her, give her that smile I know she loves and a wink she always blushed at in class. "Come. Let's paint."

My hand finds the small of her back and guides her back to her seat. There's zero fight in her. Her face doesn't even show anger. She's just…there. Present. Existing. However blank her expression might be, I know what she's really saying. Her body moves exactly where I tell it. See? This right here is exactly what I needed from all those others.

The brush fits perfectly into her little hand, exactly the way it's supposed to. My hand loops over hers and, instinctively, my chin dips into the crook of her neck. She smells like sweetness. Even her sweat is like sugar. I like it.

"You're a smart girl, Mills," I nuzzle into her neck like a puppy showing affection. "Have you figured this part out yet? Have you?"

"That you're a psychopath who's been DIYing paintbrushes using dead girls' hair?" Her voice is as silky as her hair, but her answer is not quite right. Maybe she hasn't figured it out. I lace my fingers through hers, both of us holding the paintbrush — this beautifully perfect paintbrush — together. "This isn't from a dead girl, is it?"

And it's not. She's right here, and she's giving me her all. Her *all*. Besides, I can't kill her off, not when she's so perfect. Not when she's my key. My recruit. My visionary.

She shakes her head. Maybe she doesn't believe me. Maybe she thinks she's going to end up like all those other tools. But that's all they are. Or, at least, that's all they were. Tools. Just. Tools.

But this one? Her? Well, she's something else. Something almost magical. She is the ultimate tool that I need for much, much longer.

Her eyes look glassy, almost dead. And her face is pale. Why isn't she moving? I relace my hand over hers and touch the tip to canvas.

"Paint," I whisper in her ear, and I can feel the heat of my breath bounce off her skin and land back on mine. "Show me what you can do. Help me with the final painting."

And somehow, her trance breaks again. Just enough to squeak out the words, "The final painting is done."

I look over at the one she just did. True, the last requirement with her name attached is done, but I still need mine. I still need one to put up next to hers, with my title at the bottom.

"No, love. There's still one more."

But I know where I stand in the art world. I've seen what the others at the gallery are doing, and I need to ensure that my contribution is the best of the best. And my talent? Well, it piqued ages ago, and everyone knows how the saying goes: Those that can, do. Those who can't, teach.

Together, our hands move and the brush does the work for us. There's something about the way this feels, like we've morphed into a singular being. My heart is beating with hers, and the way her facial expression is so dreamlike, I imagine she's just as curious as to where this painting is going to go as I am.

Wherever the brush — the Mills brush — takes us, it's going to be fantastic. So much better than the pudgy handler I saw at the gallery, better than his recruit, and definitely better than any of the other hacks there. This will definitely secure my seat.

"Mills." My voice shakes in my throat as I watch her splattered knuckles dance under mine. "Mills, you have ten times the talent anyone in this stupid town has, including me."

She says nothing. It's clear, her dreamlike state has swept her away, which means I'm at the wheel now. I can do anything I want with her body under my command.

But I'll hold back, because I know the second I force any movement, everything that's her will disappear within me instead of on the canvas. I can't have that. Not now. Not yet.

I use my words to coax her to continue, "It's true, you know. Since the first day you stepped foot in my classroom, I knew you were special." I take a deep breath and close my eyes, picturing her eagerness right in front of me. A young and engaging student just ready to be prepped and cared for.

It didn't matter how many girls I took from that classroom to explore. It didn't matter whose hair clippings I turned into tools. No amount of use or effort would hold a candle to this girl right here. The one in my arms dazily painting a masterpiece without any effort at all.

The brush swishes this way and that. I have no idea what it's turning into, but it's already more beautiful than all the pieces before. That's a hard feat, considering this one so far is only black. Lines and strokes fly every which way and each movement fills me with a jolt of excitement.

"And I tried, too, Mills. I tried finding someone else to compare you to, but no one else could."

Her hair smells like silk and butterflies.

"And I've tried myself. I tried to take the little bit of talent from others, take a piece of each of them and paint with the pieces of those girls. But do you know what happened?"

She says nothing. That's okay. I let my pretty do my work for me.

"Once I snippity snipped their hair, they lost everything to me. Whatever was appealing, whatever made them seem talented, whatever made them beautiful and easy to handle, it all disappeared. I couldn't look at them as talent anymore. They were just used up. They were trash. So I took care of them."

All movement stopped. She must be nervous, afraid to perform. So I need to encourage her a little.

"But not you, my love. Never you. You're far from trash. You're absolutely perfect. This is proof of that." I release my hand from hers and we gaze at her painting together. There's no mistake. It's her. It's her self-portrait done in jagged sketchy lines. Each one feels like a step into herself, into her heart, her mind, and her soul.

And it fills me with both excitement and sadness.

Then she dips her brush into the blue. I watch the pieces of her hair accept the blue as its own. It swirls in circles and mixes together until I realize it's not an average blue anymore. It's bright. Inviting.

I rip my eyes away from her movements and focus again on the black-lined painting. Oh my heart hurts at the birdcage that sits on top of her painted shoulders. She's trapped. Of course she's trapped. How could I be so stupid?

I've been so wrapped up into myself and getting my part done, I've completely forgotten to tell her the best part.

"Oh, love. I'm so sorry you have felt trapped all this time. But can I tell you a secret? You have to promise not to tell anyone I told you, though. Because you're not supposed to know, not yet."

Back to the brush. It's stopped swirling around and is now ready to do its job. Its final mark. It moves above the canvas and with a few delicate moves, it's there. The final piece. An electric blue butterfly in the cage with her.

I shake off the feeling I get when I see that butterfly and ease the brush out of her hand. I wipe it clean of every bit of blue and dip it back into the black paint to collect just the right amount to add my signature to the bottom of the painting we did together. It's so much better than I could have imagined. The message in this one surmounts anything else that could possibly be at the gallery.

"The thing is, Mills, we're all trapped here, on this plane called Planet Earth. We're stuck in these bodies, these vessels, desperately trying to tell our stories to others, wanting them to hear and feel everything inside of us. But very rarely, and I mean this sincerely, very rarely does anyone honestly understand."

"But there is good news to this, and I want you in on it. The good news is that your story doesn't have to be trapped." I ease in even closer to her, wrapping my arms over her shoulders. "There is a Dignitary out there ready to take some of us to another plane. The better plane. The plane where everyone understands each others' stories just by looking at one another. There's no fear. There's no despair. There's no entrapment from other people's stupidity. But there's only a small amount of room. Not everyone can go."

Her face changes. Her brows knit. This tells me that she's soaking in everything I'm saying. This is good. She will be on board. She'll be so willing to take the next steps with me, straight into The Circle.

"But you can help me go, Mills. You are my key. Together, we can share your story. Everyone will hear it. Everyone will see it. You'll never have to be trapped again, love."

I give her a squeeze and my entire body shutters. My eyes fall to the floor, and I'm reminded of how different this is compared to all the others. Even Katelynn, the first, the girl who left that stupid mark on the floor I could never get rid of, she is such a past memory that doesn't hold a single light to Mills. Oh, how I want to take every inch of Mills' talent for myself. But I must restrain myself. Knowing how this has to go, I need to restrain.

I loosen my grip on her and it feels like I'm letting go a piece of myself. "Mills, say something, love. I need you to know you'll never feel trapped again."

She looks up at me, doe-like eyes that have overcome their glassiness. Her dreamlike state is gone and she's completely present in front of me.

"They weren't trash."

"Huh?" Her response is puzzling.

"Those girls. They weren't trash." And then she spits in my face. "But you are."

CHAPTER TWENTY-SIX

My feet finally move on their own, and they take a step forward. "You're the trash, Noland Elsinger." I can feel myself shake, but I hold my voice steady. I don't want him to think for even a second that I'm scared of him. Horrible men aren't as terrifying as those who stand up to them. And if I have any say in how the rest of this evening goes, I won't be the next dead girl in a painting.

Not by his hands.

But him? I'll paint the entirety of Volga with his blood if I can.

"Why?" I ask him. "Why kill them? Why not be a normal shady ass man who sleeps with a girl and forgets about her? Why be an even worse human being and take their lives, too?"

"Why?" And the man has the gull to actually lean over and inch to my lips in an attempt to kiss me. His mouth is inches from mine and cocked off to the side like I had been waiting for this for a lifetime.

I haven't.

I throw my hands up and stop him. "No." Thank Vincent VanGogh I'm finally breaking out of my paralyzed state of shock and can do something about my situation.

"Careful there, Ms. Ellis. I would really, really hate for you to end up like, well, I guess like your friend." If the man could muster up puppy dog eyes, he would have, but it comes off as a weird stray who has overstayed his welcome through one too many asks. "You are so much better than them." He moves his hand up and down my arm and I step backward to inch away as best as I can from him.

He grabs my arm, and I can feel his fingertips dig into my skin. The way he's gripping, my arm will be purple by tomorrow morning, if I make it to tomorrow morning. "You deserve more, Mills. Because you can *do* more. You can *be* more."

I yank my arm away and run backward toward the supply table. My back hits the corner and I can hear something roll off the table and hit the floor. I swallow down a lump that is hanging in my throat, hoping that it wasn't one of Noland's special paint brushes.

"You, Ms. Ellis, have something I want."

"I have nothing." My hands move along the side of the table, feeling my way even further into the basement.

"You have *everything*. I want to tap into you and see where that talent is hidden. I need some of that talent for myself. With everything you have, surely you can spare some of it. Maybe I can climb inside of you and find a piece to pinch off for myself."

My feet stumble when they hit the foot of a folding chair. It knocks over and clangs loudly on the cement floor.

"None of those other girls had that. They were just… fun. They were playthings I thought would inspire me. You know how inspiration feels good? They felt good. Real good. Until they didn't. Everything flopped on the ground when what I thought was inspiration went flaccid. And I couldn't have them going around existing like their own shit didn't stink when it stank worse than anyone else's. They weren't enough." He makes a move to come after me and I dart into a corner. "They weren't *you*." His look is hungry. I'm sure he wants to devour me.

My hand finds a ruler on the table. I wrap my hand around it without taking my eyes off the madman in front of me. "They were still *people!*" I scream the last word and throw the ruler at him.

It clips his shoulder. I always had bad aim.

When he dodges my lame attack, I take the opportunity to lengthen my distance from him. While my feet dance quickly away from the table, my hands grab what they can: pens, markers, a pair of scissors, and one of his insane brushes… Livvy's brush.

For a moment, I close my eyes and say a one-second prayer that she can have my back once again. May everything I can grab work in my favor.

I go through the arsenal in my fists rapid fire as he chases me toward the back corner of the basement.

Three pens fly by his stupid smile I wish I could erase. A marker hits him in the chest and there is zero flinch. He catches the Livvy brush in his hands and that stupid smiles twists to an even more sinister look. I guess that brush means too much to him to let it drop on the dirty floor. Heaven forbid.

"I need you, Mills." Noland's voice has turned into a growl. "I need to know where your talent comes from. I need a taste… I need to open you up and lap it up like a hungry puppy. Secure everything that's meant for me." He licks his lips as he lunges toward me. And that's when I flip the scissors in my hands and jab the pointed tips out in front of me.

He lunges forward the same time I do, and we meet in the middle.

The scissors pierce his shirt. When I feel them start to resist, I plunge harder, deeper. I enter him more evasively than I will ever allow him to do to me. The sludgy sound turns my stomach as I turn the handle of the scissors, making a jagged hole of flesh under his shirt.

He yells.

Sorry, no, he doesn't yell. He *screams*. And in a way, it's so delightful to hear.

I want him to scream more. I want him to feel every bit of pain all those girls felt.

Still holding the scissors, I open them. They resist some more, but I use all my hand strength to open them as wide as they can while inside his chest. I picture that hole widening more, allowing his evil to drip out so I can paint with it and show the world what he's really made of.

It's a shame I have bad aim. I wanted to hit his left side. Missing his heart was a problem on my end. I make a note to myself to practice my aim for the next time I end up in some dank basement with a horrible man.

He screams again, like a little girl, but whinier, and backs up. Noland has such a quick moment of shock that I'm jealous he can recover and get back to what he's after: Me.

Noland grasps at the scissor handles and yanks them out from his shirt. It only takes a few seconds before the right front of his shirt turns a dark red.

"Let me see it!" he yells as he lunges.

Adrenaline must be a fantastic pain reliever because both he and I are moving like wildcats without issue. I jump to the side to avoid his lunge. My voice finds its way out into the open, too. "You'll never see where my talent is!"

If I'm being honest, I don't really know what that means. Just moments ago, he was talking crazy talk about being selected for some kind of group or circle or…

Memento Mori Society.

Or a cult.

I dodge him again as he leaps toward me and I leap away. Only now, I'm stuck in a freaking corner and he is only feet away, ready to close in and do whatever it is his pervy and twisted mind has in store.

I don't care. I have the strength of me, of Livvy, and of every girl he ever raped and killed within me. I can feel them cheering me on as I say in the most stable voice I've ever used, "You'll never know talent, because you've never had talent."

And it's true. He even said so himself. He taught art because he could never actually succeed in doing art himself. What a lame reason to be a professor.

The look in his face shifts. Something hits him and his entire body changes. He's no longer a careful man, taking in every moment in front of him. His eyes tell me he's ready to throw all caution to the wind and grab at me in any way possible. I can see his fist clench. But as his fist swings forward, I roll to the side and escape the punch that hits the wall. My foot trips over his when I roll. I fall to the ground. My knees hit so hard, I can feel them scrape under my jeans.

My favorite jeans that I saved from the washing machine from hell just a floor above me. How I wish I could make my way back up there now, get away from this hack and run out into the open, deliver the message of the girls before me and warn all the girls who would have been after me.

On hands and knees, I crawl away from him. I only get a foot or so past his stance before I feel his hand around my ankle and pull me back.

My body skids across the floor back to him and I can feel every piece of gravel in the cement under me dig across my skin. For a split second, a spec of electric blue flies past my eyes, and all I can think of is who that might have come from, which girl of the past might have left her mark here, leaving me a message I didn't understand.

The Summer Girl.

With all my strength, I kick for her. Kicking does nothing but make his grip even tighter.

He flips me over and works his way up, holding both of my wrists down with his hands and prying my legs wide with his knees. When he shimmies his pants down, something flies out of his pocket and across the floor. I can't see where it lands, but it doesn't matter. I can smell the metallic blood on his shirt, and even though I know the wound underneath must hurt while it slowly drains out his life, Noland doesn't show any sign of pain or fatigue. His eyes are searching deep within mine and his mouth reads that he's ready to take what was never his to have. My *talent*.

I scream and cry. I scramble to get away, but every movement I make, he makes his hold even stronger. I can feel the bruises forming under my skin. I can't breathe. I can't move. I can't figure out how to get away from under his grasp.

This is what those girls must have felt. In this moment, I'm living their stories. It's not just an inspired guess. It's real. And I hate it. I never wanted this. Not for them and not for myself. They must have been scared and vulnerable. They must have fallen for his stupid charming facade only to realize how much bullshit it really was. I look into his eyes the way I hoped every single one of the girls he violated, alive and dead, looked at him: With disgust, knowing that one day, he'll meet his match.

I will do what I can to be that match.

I move one arm up, the other across. Right now, it's doing nothing but holding myself in place.

I move one knee in front of him and push his stomach away. This is better. I feel stronger, in control. My other foot lands on his hip, and in one swift motion, I push and roll.

I am away. I'm free. And the gas range is in front of me. My body races toward it as fast as it can take me. It's not fast, but it's quick enough. I can feel his hands hit the ground behind me. They're slapping in a rhythm I'm only slightly faster than.

My legs scramble under me and I push up to a standing position. A miracle has brought me to the bottom of the stairs, but I'm not going up them yet. I know if I do, he'll only chase me, and I want to prevent that from happening as much as possible.

Something shiny is on the ground, about the size of my thumb, and oh my gosh, it's somehow perfect and heartbreaking and exhilarating all in one.

It's Noland's lighter. It must have been the thing that fell out of his pocket.

Before I can second guess myself, I scoop it from the ground and flick it open. All I can see now is the tiny flame in front of me and the gas stove that's going to grow that flame into something much, much bigger. It's time to go out with a bang.

This one is for you, Liv.

Biting my lip, I hope my aim is finally good enough, because it needs to be. It has to be.

I take one last look into his eyes and smile. "So long, sucker."

The lighter flies from my hand, straight to the gas burner behind Noland. His face is memorable, and I can only hope that I'll burn the gratification of his fear and desperation to memory before the whole place explodes.

CHAPTER TWENTY-SEVEN

Livvy

Woo-sah. Boy, does my head hurt, a lot. It's a good thing Doctor Crane found me on the street during his run, and came back with cold water, a towel, and Tylenol. I'm pretty sure anyone else would have left me for a goner. I smile up at him and he smiles back. I used to agree with Mills. His eyes are beady and his nose hooks like a cartoonish villain. It does make him look a little untrustworthy. But there's kindness in his smile and I appreciate that. Which is exactly why I didn't want to believe the rumors against him.

Boy, do I appreciate it.

"Doctor Crane, I want to thank you."

He waves his hand to brush off the appreciation. "No thanks needed. I'm happy to help."

A little laugh escapes me. "Well, my life kinda depended on that help, so I'm pretty sure I owe you at the very least a thanks."

"Then I guess you're welcome."

We sit in a small silence together. I'm sure he knows I'm the best friend of the former student who called him out for something he didn't do. And I'm sure he feels just as awkward as I do sitting in his office without having much to say.

"Say, why were you out there anyway? It's not like Deuces is known for professors hanging out in that area or whatever. Don't you all kind of avoid places that are a little too rowdy?"

Crane crosses his arms. "Don't you think that might be the exact reason why I was there?"

I feel my eyebrows bend into confusion. "I don't get it."

"Look, I know what you kids think of me. Everyone does at first. They say I'm a cranky old man who's got nothing better to do than… well, some pretty unspeakable things." He swallows back what I'm assuming are some defensive words he'd rather not say out loud. "But the truth is, I watch over you kids. This year in particular, I've made it my job. I have to ever since…" His voice tails off. His mind is elsewhere.

"Ever since what, professor?"

"Last Summer. My niece was accepted into Volga. In her excitement, she came to scope out the campus. She was hoping to sneak into the dorms to check them out and meet some of the professors. She wanted to get to know who she would be working with, where she'd be living. She wanted to learn about her new home. But then.." He swallows back again.

I don't want to pry. I don't know what he was about to say, but clearly it's sensitive. I move the ice from my temple to put my hand on his arm. I notice on his desk is a framed photo of a young girl. Her elbows are on the table in front of her and her hands are clasped together by her cheek. Each finger interlocks, with a pattern of cream skin and electric blue nail polish. The name Katelynn Abercross is printed at the bottom. Abercross doesn't sound familiar, but her pointed nose sure is recognizable. Genes are funny like that. Sometimes people look more like their uncles than their actual parents.

He shrugs my hand off as well as whatever emotions were about to overtake him. "That's another story for another time," he continues. "The point is, that's why I take to all those girls. I know they stay out late, they go to the parties, they have whatever drinks and fun they want. I can't stop them from any of that. But if I can keep an eye out for them and teach a little self defense, I feel like I've done my job." He takes another breath. "So, yeah, that's why I was over at Deuces. Once in a while, I meander over there just to check things out. Stay aware. Tell the girls who come to my office that I understand the situations they end up in, and design lessons just for that."

Another nervous laugh escapes me. "So I guess I'm one of those lessons, Professor Crane?"

He adjusts his stance a bit nervously. "Every student is a lesson, Ms. Landon. I just hope I don't have to teach yours to anyone else."

My jaw tightens and the sting of tears threatens to creep into the open. I know what he means. He's talking about all the girls. All the ones in Mills's paintings.

The one in the photo on his desk. Katelynn. His niece. The Summer Girl.

"Professor Crane, I need to tell you something." He's proven he's worthy of trust. I can share what I know with him. "How I ended up there-"

Crane perks up. All of a sudden, he's eager for the truth and for justice. "I was hoping you'd tell me what happened. You don't seem like the kind of student to get caught wandering around outside of frat houses and alleyways. You're too smart."

I see what he did there.

"Well, I guess you're right because I wasn't there for any of that. But I was there for my friend."

"Oh, I think I know the one you're talking about. The one who made that painting of me?"

"Mills, yeah…" I let my voice trail off. I figured he wouldn't like talking about her. "You know, she wanted to apologize to you. I guess she hasn't done that yet, huh?"

He shakes his head. "No, she hasn't, but that's not really your call. Besides, I get it. She was just trying to do what she thought was right, regardless of how unconventional her methods are. Anyway, you were there for her?"

"Yeah. See, I've been doing some research on… beans."

"Beans?"

"Beans!"

"I see."

"Well, I found out that some beans like kidney and fava have glycosides in them. In certain conditions, if you eat too many, you can have a toxic reaction to them."

"So, they're poisonous?"

"Yes. But I also found out that most other beans can't make you sick unless you keep them out at room temperature for too long. After only a couple of hours, they can grow harmful bacteria and you can end up sitting on the porcelain throne for longer than you'd like." I'm aware my voice is going about a million miles a minute, so I do my best to slow down for the next part.

"But there is another bean that can be very poisonous, and not just in certain biological circumstances. It doesn't matter what your body composition is, how healthy your immune system, or if you have a rare blood disorder or not. This bean can do some serious damage to anyone and everyone if you're not careful."

Professor Crane looks at me with a little more interest. I'm not sure if he's completely following me or not.

"Castor beans, professor."

"Castor beans," he repeats. Then he says, "I don't follow."

So I elaborate. "Castor beans. Most people don't eat castor beans because, well, they just flat out taste nasty. But also, they contain what's called ricin inside of them. Since most people don't use the bean itself but castor oil, for things like laxatives and hair serum, most people don't realize how dangerous they really are. However, if you are making your own oil from the castor bean, all of the powdery waste material left over contains the ricin, making the powder a pretty dangerous substance in itself."

"So what does this have to do with your friend, Ms. Landon?"

"Do you know what Professor Elsinger has been teaching his students, Professor Crane?"

He shakes his head.

"He's been teaching them how to clean his special paint brushes."

"Makes sense as an art professor."

"Do you know what he's been cleaning them with?"

He shakes his head again.

"Castor oil."

He pauses. No shake of the head.

"Homemade castor oil."

His eyes seem to understand.

"So, if Professor Elsinger has been boiling down his own castor beans to make oil for his students, he's bound to have a collection of powdery poison somewhere. And the worst part of it? There's no antidote for it. None. So if he were to, say, pour some into a glass of water or beer or jungle juice to drink… It wouldn't be difficult to spike someone's solo cup or water bottle or anything. Then they would…" I let the end of that thought dangle. I don't want to actually say it.

"So then you think all those girls…?"

"I know, sir. I know those girls are connected. Because I was going over to tell Mills just that. I was going to let her know what I found out. She is so invested in their stories, and she's so close to him." I stop and collect my composure. "I'm scared, sir. I'm scared that Mills is in trouble."

Just then, I hear a loud bang, an explosion in the distance. It shocks me to the core. And somehow, my heart forgets to beat for a moment. Two. I have to will it to start again to finish my story.

"Sir, Professor Elsinger found me on the way to Mills's house."

Professor Crane nods, as if he's recalling his own version of the memory.

"He told me I looked tired. And I was. I was hot. In the heat like this, of course I was hot. He gave me a water bottle and I knew, I knew he had added some of his ricin powder in it. So I did what I thought was the brave thing. I confronted him."

I gulp at the next part. "Only, I don't know if it really was the right thing to do. He grabbed my hair, pulled it back, and tried to force me to drink that stupid bottle of water. Honestly, I think it was meant for Mills, and I just got in the way. Somehow, I knocked it out of his hand. It spilled everywhere, and he got mad. Real mad."

I look Professor Crane in the eyes. "Sir, he grabbed me by the throat. It hurt. A lot. But I swear, when I was gasping for breath, his expression changed."

"Changed?" Professor Crane swallows back words I'm sure he's saving for Professor Elsinger later.

"Yeah. It was like he went from deathly angry to scared. He looked around, like he was looking out for someone who might be watching. And even though no one else was around, his scared look didn't go anywhere. So he pushed me down with one hand and yanked out a chunk of my hair with the other. When I fell, I hit my head on the corner of that dumpster. I have no idea what happened after that until you woke me up." I shake my head at the thought of it. "I know it was stupid. I shouldn't have confronted him like that."

Professor Crane's mouth gapes open. "Ms. Landon, you're not stupid. You may have saved your own life there without even knowing it. I'm so glad you told me all this, too. It all makes sense now. Now I know who I was trying to chase down after seeing you. I know why he seems so scared, darting away like he did. But I couldn't chase him forever. Not knowing that you were there, waiting for the help I knew I could provide."

I screw my mouth up because as insane as what I'm about to say sounds, it's true. "I still don't really know what's going on. My head hurts, one of my professors is attacking girls, and I'm scared for my best friend's life."

From outside of Professor Crane's office, sirens sound off. I can't tell if they're ambulances or firetrucks or what, but they're getting louder, closer.

Right when I'm about to speak again, my purse sounds off. My phone is ringing. I dig inside the little black bag and dig it out. It's Stark.

"Livvy. Livvy are you okay?" He sounds exhausted. The sirens are even louder over the phone.

"Yeah, Stark. I'm okay. What's going on?"

"I was coming to see Mills, but her house is…" He pauses. "Her house is…" He can't seem to get it out. "Livvy, her house is on fire."

"What?"

"Livvy, the place is gone, and I'm pretty sure Mills was inside."

Everything inside of me stops moving. My heart refuses to pump blood into my veins and I can even picture how my lungs completely stop in mid-inhale. Mills was inside? Mills was inside. Mills. Was. Inside.

Inside her burning house. Inside. Her. House.

None of these words make sense. None of them settle well with me. And all I can wonder is if Professor Elsinger was anywhere near her at the time.

Mills couldn't be hurt. She can't. She's the strongest person I know. If she were inside a burning house with a predator trapped inside with her, then she would scrap her way out of it. I'm sure.

"Stark," I manage out.

"Yeah?" His voice is cracking, too.

"Stark, I know Mills. If she was in there, she's not dead."

She can't be. There's no way that girl would allow herself to be taken away like that.

"Livvy, this place is a mess. It was a huge explosion. I don't know how anyone could survive that. If she was in there..." I can tell he's terrified and doesn't have any stock in what I'm saying, but I say it anyway. My gut instincts tell me I need to.

"Stark, Mills isn't dead. We have to find her."

A REVIEW REQUEST

Thank you so much for dedicating some of your time to get to know the characters who have been with me for so long. If you enjoyed this book, please take a few minutes to rate and review Paint by Murders on Goodreads or Amazon.

Even a few words help others decide if this is the book meant for them.

***

Your Book is Lonely!

Please consider adding a few friends on your shelf!

Emily Ellis Thrillers
Paint by Murders
Paper Machete
Majestic Corpse

Other Books by Amanda Jaeger
The Fallen in Soura Heights
BreathTaken

ABOUT THE AUTHOR

Amanda Jaeger: Murderino mom of two, professional word nerd by day and author by trade.

She's the wife of her college sweetheart, and the mother of two spitfire girls, but she's also been a sign language interpreter, transcriptionist, and a book slinger. Working with words isn't her job, it's her career.

Thank goodness writing thrillers come naturally to her.

Amanda refuses to start her day without the perfect cup of coffee and a cuddle with her poodles. She also wants to let you know that poodles aren't as prissy as they seem, and they are, in fact, made of teeth, nails, and heads as hard as steel.

Residing in Virginia, you can bet on Amanda listening to true crime podcasts, watching cold case documentaries, and playing with her kids. (Not simultaneously).

And even though Amanda kinda sucks at keeping up with social media trends, she loves connecting one-on-one with readers.

You can connect with Amanda:

Text "ThrillerRead" to: (844) 495-1120

ACKNOWLEDGEMENTS

Holy crap, I hope I don't forget anyone. It takes a village, y'all. It's just as true for paperback babies as it is for the real life sticky ones. (And yes, kids are sticky.) So please bear with me, and if you made it this far in this book, then keep on reading. These people are my village to have helped make this trilogy the crazy semi-beast it is.

Before I head into it, let me clear the air that ALL MISTAKES ARE MIIIINE.

Hey YOU, yes you. The person reading this. Thank YOU. You're the reason why I write and continue to write, even when it seems a little bonkers for me to do so. The characters and stories may start with me, but you're what keeps them alive for much, much longer.

To the real life Mariëtte, who really is one of those people who you never know what's hidden beneath the surface. Thank you for being my number 1 Alpha. You're always there to help me find the gaps when my brain is fried. And without you, I'd probably get every forensic scene 1,000% wrong.

To allllll the betas: Anna, Danielle, Jamie, Carmen, and Sam. Thank you for helping me refine the details, close the gaps even further, and sometimes rearranging the cluster in my head to make more sense on paper.

The Thriller Babes: You know who you are. Out of the entire writers' community, you are the pillar that keeps me standing when the frustrations run high. Your help, guidance, expertise, and self-deprecating memes are everything I ever wanted in a peer mentorship. Thank you!

My editor, Genevieve… good grief, I couldn't do this without you. Thank you so much for helping me clean things up as I learn and relearn what the heck grammar is all about. (You'd think as an English major I would have had some kind of grammar class… but nah.)

Troy! You're stuck with me. Forever. Deal with it. Thank you for always knowing exactly how to take my insane descriptions and translate them into visuals. I know they say "Don't judge a book by its cover," but we all know that's the first thing people judge a book by. Your cover designs make my first impressions better.

To my husband, Michael, for always being supportive of my crazy writing "hobby" (slash work slash obsession). Because of you, I have the time, space, and love to actually create the stories that keep me (us) up all night.

My kids, who keep asking what the heck I'm writing about but aren't allowed to yet read it. I know you two have snuck a few peeks over my shoulder. I'm not mad, but I'll definitely understand if you need therapy later. Love you to pieces.

And the rest of my family who continue to be supportive both loudly and quietly. Thank you for reading when you want, loving me even when you don't want to read what I write, and smiling when I talk too much about it. THANK YOU FOR BEING YOU.

Made in the USA
Monee, IL
09 May 2023

33384145R10132